Feelings for Rebar resurface as Cameo recalls all that's happened. But she can't trust that Camille is out of his life. During a long road trip to South Dakota, tornados rumble across the Midwest and Malika makes a play for Cameo's trust along the way.

White Wolf warns the members of Ricochet that a dark spirit haunts Malika making her extremely dangerous. The group seeks to break the supernatural connection she's established with Shook.

Rush feels left out during Cameo's time of discovery. His patience and strength are tested. Rebar has a violent clash with an unexpected visitor. And Malika drops a bombshell on Cameo that rocks everyone's world.

On the Trail of Feathers
Copyright © 2023 Shiloh Love
ISBN: 978-1-4874-4053-4
Cover art by Martine Jardin

Published by eXtasy Books Inc

Look for us online at:
www.eXtasybooks.com

ON THE TRAIL OF FEATHERS
FEATHER BLUE 7

BY

SHILOH LOVE

CHAPTER ONE

Cameo hummed along to a song on the radio while organizing groceries in the fridge. A week had flown by since the standoff in Amarillo, leaving little time to complete her move away from Denver unless she wanted to pay another month's rent.

Rush made it quite clear that he wanted her to move in with him and suggested she have movers place her belongings into a nearby storage unit until she made up her mind. He expressed concern for her safety with Malika out there somewhere. He also worried about the trauma she'd endured the past several weeks and her overall wellbeing.

From the day Rebar chased her down in early May, chaos had dominated her life. Hostility from his former friends, Camille's resentment, Malika's involvement, the General's threatening presence, and then the final standoff, had caused one stress factor after another.

She felt safe staying in Rush's Dallas County ranch home with half the Ricochet family. Stoke, Rider and Shook decided to hang out with her and Rush while the situation involving Camille, Shade, and possibly Malika, was still very much uncertain.

Rebar, Chamber and Levi were staying with Moss in his Denton County home less than an hour away. She wondered how Rebar was settling in with his new friends. He'd been unmistakably clear that he was done with Camille. But the question hanging heavy on the air — was Camille done with him?

Cameo hadn't had a single moment or spare braincell to put toward seeking a job yet, given all that happened since her return to the States. Rush's sincere invitation seemed the most logical and peaceful way to go, especially with their growing feelings toward one another. She wanted to take it slow with Rush, though. Both were fully aware she had unresolved feelings over the breakup with Rebar. She wasn't ready to take their budding relationship to the next level, but Rush seemed okay with their current status and arrangement.

What she'd thought she had with Rebar had blown up in her face, shattering the new life she'd tried to build in Colorado. Now the Mile High state held nothing but bad memories — and her belongings.

"Hey, angel." Rush peeked his head around the door. "We're just right outside tuning up the bikes. Wanna get it done before dark. You doing okay in here?"

"Yeah, I'm good." She smiled adoringly at him. He was so attentive. Rebar had perhaps given her too much space. Then again, Rebar hadn't conquered his own demons before dragging her into his wreckage. "I'm enjoying the music and organizing the kitchen. Maybe I'll even cook," she teased with a playful wink.

"You don't have to cook. We can order takeout or toss steaks on the grill. I want you to relax, settle in, enjoy the feeling of home." He walked over and took her in his arms. "Chill with us."

"Okay." She accepted his sweet kiss. "I'll join you guys on the patio when you're finished."

"That's my girl." He flashed a charming smile, kissed her again then strolled back out the kitchen door.

Yes, this definitely feels right, she told herself. *Tomorrow I'll call the movers and have them place my stuff in the storage facility Rush recommended. I want to be here with him where it's safe and calm.* The past week with him had been a much-needed reprieve.

She glanced out the small window above the sink. A beautiful sunset lit the western horizon with warm hues of gold and blue. Texas seemed like a fabulous state thus far, with plenty of fun things to do, breathtaking landscapes and the ocean was only about four hours away.

Rush and his three buddies were cleaning the bikes after doing maintenance on them. She loved how he meticulously took care of his ranch and everything he owned. He was a hands-on kind of guy—ruggedly handsome with irresistible sex appeal. She reminded herself to guard her heart a little better this time, no matter how sexy these Damocles brothers were.

She heard them fire up the bikes to park them around back for the night.

She finished lining rows of ice cream pints in the freezer, then took one last look at everything. Satisfied with her work, she grabbed packs of fresh steak from the fridge and headed for the patio to wait for the guys. She thought about surprising Rush by preparing the grill and having the steaks sizzling by the time they returned.

Before she left the kitchen, her keen sense of smell picked up the scent of distinct perfume—a familiar fruity blend with strong rose notes. She stopped in her tracks but didn't turn around.

No way.

"Cameo," a soft voice called, sounding very close.

"Nope. I'm having a flashback," she muttered to herself.

"No, darling. You're not imagining me. I'm really here."

As if compelled, against her better judgment, Cameo spun around to look at the owner of the familiar voice. Her jaw dropped slightly, and her eyes widened.

Now I know I'm having a flashback.

There before her stood Malika, barely clothed in a skinny strapless black dress slit up the side to her hip. She wore an elaborate feathered headdress typically reserved for

3

chieftains, but in some strange way, it worked for her. The colorful array of feathers evinced femininity and coordinated with the passionate blue paint on her forehead, shoulders, and neck. Light purple rouged her high cheekbones. White streaks trailed from her lower lash line and lower lip. Other white markings, which bore no specific pattern, accented her bare shoulders and face.

The lines drawn down from her eyes struck a familiar chord in Cameo's memory. They resembled the lines Shook had painted on his face while undercover.

Oh my gosh. She's declared war on Shook.

"What do you want?" Cameo asked, still not convinced this was real.

"To see my daughter," she replied sweetly. "And to let you know how proud I am of you."

"Proud of me? Since when?" Cameo scoffed.

"You protected your sister. Even though she didn't deserve it, you took the strike meant for her, then covered her with your coat. The way you stood off with the General was nothing short of heroic. I was ashamedly wrong about you, Cameo."

Cameo thought for a minute. *How could Malika know that I threw my jacket over Camille when she launched the teargas during the shootout?* Her mind flashed back to the recent sting op by Ricochet to arrest the General and his cohorts. *Oh, she's probably already paid Camille a visit. More than likely, my twin filled her in. I'm in a daze. This isn't real.*

"Okay," Cameo said, leaning against the counter. "I'm just gonna roll with this one. I know this is an illusion because you'd never say those things."

"I've come to warn you, child. War is on the horizon. Shade is furious with Rebar and Ricochet for taking out the General. He's organizing his troop." Malika held out her hand, palm facing up. "Join us, darling. Leave this pack of renegades and choose the winning team."

"*You're* the one who killed the General *and* Missy. Doesn't Shade know the truth?"

A smug grin touched her red-painted lips. "He's a man. Does he deserve the truth?"

"Not all men are the enemy."

"Hm. Perhaps one day you will understand." She extended her other hand. Something blue rested on the palm. "Take it, darling. It'll guard your heart."

"A feather?" Cameo stared at the sky-blue plume resting on her mother's hand.

"I've given you no reason to trust me," Malika said, tears in her large black eyes. "Please trust me just once and accept this rare gift for protection. Show it to no one."

Cameo reached out and took the feather into her hand. "I'm not afraid of Shade or anyone associated with him. You killed the one man I feared. And I guess I should thank you for that. But no more fighting, Mother. I've found my place here. I'm tired of all the drama. It's not why I came to the US."

"Shook betrayed me! Do you not have any loyalty to your own mother?" Anger flared in her black eyes.

Okay...this is getting intense, Cameo thought. *I'm not gonna let it go any further.* Her muscles tensed. "You shouldn't be here. You're not here! You're only in my mind! Get the hell out!" Cameo shouted.

At that moment, Rush and Shook burst into the kitchen. Cameo saw Malika stiffen, her gaze drifting straight to Shook and fixating on him. "You..." She tilted her head. "You were a naughty, naughty boy...but you *are* still gorgeous..." Sadness swept over her exquisite face, followed by fury.

"And you're a wanted criminal," Shook stated coldly, then advanced toward her.

Malika raised one arm then whipped something at their feet. A plume of blue smoke rose from the floor. The cloud smelled faintly of wild roses. Then, without a sound, she was gone—just gone.

Cameo staggered backward as Shook and Rush combed the immediate area. She closed her hand around the feather.

"Rider! Stoke!" Rush yelled.

The two men bolted through the door into the kitchen. "What's going on?" Stoke asked.

"Malika. Stay with Halo while we search the house," Rush told them, then he and Shook took off.

"Are you okay, babe?" Stoke wrapped a comforting arm around her shoulders.

"I-I think so...I thought I was having a flashback. Am I?" She felt bewildered.

"No, sweetheart. You're okay," Rider assured her.

"I need some water." She reached into the fridge and grabbed a bottle then stood silently with the two men, waiting for Rush and Shook.

"What's that blue mist?" Rider looked around curiously. "Smells like...flowers."

"Malika. It's like she has some kind of magic. She was dressed really odd, like she was going to a costume party." Cameo described her mother's appearance to them while it was still fresh in her mind. Then she told them word for word what her mother had said before she forgot, just in case this was really a flashback.

"Good thing we were right outside," Stoke said. "We heard you shouting at someone. Rush told us to wait until he and Shook went in to see what was going on. We usually work that way. Keeping a couple guys on the downlow gives us an edge over surprises."

"So that's why I didn't see the two of you at the General's hellhole?"

Rider nodded. "Stoke and I are kind of like dark horses. We don't enter the race until we're needed if that makes sense."

"Plus, we can cover the exits and catch perps off guard,"

Stoke added.

"I appreciate the calm conversation," she told them, realizing they were keeping her grounded.

"No worries. We've got your back." Rider gave her a wink. "Gotta protect our angel."

His comment drew a smile to her lips. She began to feel the tension leave her body and waited calmly with them until Rush and Shook returned. They'd been searching the house and grounds for half an hour.

"Nothing," Shook said when they finally came back.

"It's like she vanished in that puff of smoke," Rush said with a shake of his head. "Are you okay, angel?" He took her into his arms.

"I think so." She clung to him, breathing in his scent, a mix of subtle cologne and light sweat, drowning out the rose fragrance.

"Did she say anything?" Rush asked.

Cameo repeated every detail as she had to the others. She felt relief over remembering, for that fact alone distinguished this incident from her blackouts of which she had no recollection.

"The paint on her face," Cameo began. "Most notably the lines drawn down from her eyes... Like she was copycatting Shook. I believe she's declared war on him or something."

"That's gratitude for ya," quipped Shook. "Risked my life twice to save her and she turns on me."

"She doesn't handle rejection well."

Shook let out a short sardonic laugh. "Most women don't. But I've never dealt with one this extreme."

Rush led everyone outside to the patio. He tossed the steaks on the grill then plopped onto a two-seater chaise. Cameo went to him and cuddled onto the chair and crawled under his protective arm. Malika's appearance troubled her and had disrupted the peace she'd found.

"I can't believe that woman managed to evade eight skilled, fully armed men in Amarillo." Rush sighed. "It's embarrassing."

"Don't be embarrassed," she told him. "Ricochet couldn't possibly grasp the full extent of Malika's wrath or capabilities. I'm not sure what organizations she was affiliated with, but I got the impression they weren't legal."

"She and the General were into some heavy stuff," Shook informed them. "Human trafficking, paternity tampering, untraceable drugs, multiple homicide. They were more than common criminals. With him gone, it's hard to tell what her next move will be."

"I'd put my money on Shade. That's who she came to warn me about." Cameo cast an apprehensive look around the group.

"Possibly," Shook agreed with a shrug. "But she's tapped into some powerful Lakota medicine. From what I know of Shade, he's strictly military. He wouldn't dabble in her kind of trickery."

"I agree." Rush walked the few feet to the grill and pulled the steaks. "If Shade decides to wage war on Ricochet, he won't likely use a woman to help him."

"Then how would Malika know what Shade's thinking?"

"Maybe they're having an affair," Rider suggested.

"That would explain why Malika sent Camille after Rebar and why Shade went along with it," Shook noted.

Rush handed everyone a plate loaded with a still sizzling Ribeye, then sat back down with Cameo. "Rebar did tell us Shade was attracted to your mother."

"Wouldn't that go against military laws or something?" she asked.

"He's no longer on active duty. There's no law governing who a soldier takes to bed. Abetting a wanted felon is a whole different story. It all depends on how far Shade let his

8

attraction go and if he'll continue to act on it," Rush said,

"He might be a dick but he's still human," Stoke scoffed.

"True," Cameo agreed. "I just can't see Shade falling that far, though. He seemed like a rock the few times I met him."

Stoke shrugged. "We don't know the man. He must have some flaws for half his men to abandon him."

"Obviously," Cameo said with light sarcasm. "He let his fiancée sleep with Rebar on some insane spy mission. But we're way off track here. Malika is probably more dangerous than Shade could ever be. I don't know much about her, only what she told me during our few times together. Most of that was just her backstory about the General. He's gone now. So, what is she up to? Why the dramatic costume and paint? And what's this Lakota medicine you mentioned?" She really was curious over Shook's mention of it and how he even knew.

Unease flitted through his dark eyes. "I don't like talking about it, but for you, I will. Only because I know you will relate. Remember we told you that Ricochet is made up of outcasts, wanderers, and rebels who want justice?"

She thought back. "Yes, I remember."

"I'm a half-breed, Halo. My father, a full-blooded Lakota, was in love with a white woman. She was from an affluent white family that didn't approve of mixed marriage. When she got pregnant with me, they forced her to give me up for adoption because of my race, then they moved away."

Halo gasped, partly in shock and partly in sadness. "I'm so sorry. I didn't mean to—"

"No, it's okay. I'm a grown man. I'm over it." He offered her a reassuring smile.

"Did you ever meet your birth parents?" She felt a new connection with him as their past shared similar threads.

"No. My birthmother never tried to contact me, and I was told by the Tribal Council that my father disappeared."

"Who raised you? I hope I'm not being too nosy."

"Not at all. The guys here know my past. This is my family now, has been for twenty years. I'm an original Ricochet member."

"Ah, so that's how you became Rush's wingman," she said, putting a few missing pieces together. She knew very little about Shook.

He nodded and smiled. "In answer to your question, I was raised by a Lakota Medicine Man. White Wolf lived off the rez so it was acceptable. The Nation frowns on half-breeds. Whites don't want us either. But the Tribal Council allowed him to take me in since he had his own private cabin in a remote area."

"What about school?" she asked.

"Didn't get much of that so I joined the military at seventeen. I got my GED and worked on furthering my education. I developed a strong interest in law enforcement, and I excelled in school. The Bureau offered me a job after I had served eight years in the service. They liked my attitude and said my physical appearance was ideal for an undercover agent. So there ya have it. Half-breed Shook turned Fed," he concluded with a light laugh.

She loved his genuine smile. His attitude was indeed remarkable. He'd opened up about a difficult upbringing in a realistic mature manner without a hint of self-pity. She easily saw why Rush had warmed to him and that's how he became his closest comrade.

"Does Shook have a last name?" she asked.

"He does." Shook cast her a wink and gave her that beguiling smile again.

"Okay." She felt herself blush. "I get it. Sorry for prying."

"No worries, babe. Thanks for understanding."

"I do, more than you think. I truly love that Ricochet gave me the name Halo. I needed to separate myself from my upbringing."

Shook arched one brow as if impressed. "You *do* get it."

"Yeah." She returned his smile, feeling more a part of the family every day. "I imagine you know a great deal about the Lakota way having been raised by a Medicine Man."

"White Wolf is a wise man. I wouldn't say I know a lot, though. I haven't been in touch with him since I left. What I remember most is that he loved telling stories. His eyes would light up while regaling me with tales of my ancestors and legends. He lived in a white man's world but upheld his Lakota beliefs in the privacy of his cabin deep in the South Dakota hills."

"Sounds fascinating."

"I was lonely. No friends, no family, other than the old man who agreed to raise me. He worked me hard. I didn't mind, though. He was frail and needed a strong buck to chop wood and do maintenance. I think that's why the Council agreed to let him have me. They knew he would need a handyman as he got older."

"You have an admirable outlook."

He shrugged with an easy smile. "Hard work's good for a man."

"Do you think he's still alive?" she dared to ask.

"Last I checked he was. Why?"

"Maybe he'd know what Malika is doing or have some clues for us. Can you take us to him?"

Shook glanced at Rush, who gave a slight nod.

"You feel up to a fifteen-hour road trip on the back of a Harley, babe?" Shook asked her.

"Sounds wonderful. I'd love to snuggle up behind Rush on his awesome bike again."

Rider smiled, seemingly pleased by her enthusiasm. "Perfect season for a ride up to South Dakota. Remember our pilgrimage to Sturgis?"

"That was wild." Shook laughed. "But we're not headed

up that far this time. Pine Ridge is just across the southern border."

"Once was enough for me," Rush said. "Either way, you're right, the weather's great for a ride."

"I'm in," added Stoke. "We could all use some downtime."

"Should we rally the other four?" Rush looked around their circle.

No one replied right away as they contemplated his question. They seemed to be waiting for Shook's response.

Cameo discreetly observed the four handsome men while finishing her steak.

"I'd rather not take the probie up to White Wolf's place. Rebar might have eyes on him," Shook finally replied. "Namely Shade and his cohorts. I don't wanna put White Wolf in their crosshairs."

"True," Rush agreed. "We're less likely to be followed if it's just the four of us."

Stoke and Rider nodded in agreement.

Cameo felt the same. "No argument from me. I could use a break from all the drama."

"Alrighty then," Rush said. "Looks like we're on for a fun ride. Let's get the bikes packed. We'll head out tomorrow."

CHAPTER TWO

Cameo packed light as per Rush's instructions. Before leaving for their road trip, she made sure to schedule movers to finish packing up her apartment and haul everything down to a climate-controlled storage facility a few miles from Rush's home.

She was excited about her first real adventure on a Harley. Her first rides had been fast, short, and disastrous. This time, she'd get to see some great American scenery and visit a genuine Medicine Man. She couldn't deny that Shook's Lakota heritage fascinated her, as she was also half Lakota. Everything about this road trip excited her.

Rush told her she could take one backpack. Fortunately, her extensive work history in forestry and wildlife prepared her for this. She was accustomed to traveling with the bare minimum if necessary. After doublechecking her leather bag to make sure she had the essentials, she slung it over one shoulder and trotted downstairs to join the guys.

"I don't believe it," Rush said when she walked up to him in the living room. He, Stoke, and Rider stared at her in visible surprise.

"What? What?" She turned in circles inspecting herself, thinking something was showing that shouldn't be.

"You actually have just *one* bag," he said with a laugh of disbelief.

"That's what you told me to bring," she countered with pointed brows. "Was I supposed to pack more?"

He laughed in adoring amusement. "No, sugar. I just

didn't think you could do it."

She flattened her hand against his chest and gave him a playful shove. "Ha. Never underestimate me." With a proud smile, she marched past them into the kitchen, then looked back. "Well? Are you guys coming? I'm ready to roll."

They chuckled and grinned at her.

"We're right behind you," Stoke said.

Outside, she gawked at their Harleys—four very impressive, gleaming black machines loaded with chrome and accented with fringed leather saddlebags stood waiting. Rush's bike displayed a nice backrest on the passenger seat.

They straddled the bikes, revved the engines, and headed out onto the highway. Their route would take them due north, straight through the middle of Oklahoma and Kansas, then doglegging northwest across Nebraska and just over the southwest corner of South Dakota to a place called Pine Ridge. Three more states she could add to her list she'd see in America.

She was relieved they wouldn't be riding all the way up to Sturgis. She'd heard about that rally and didn't think she'd fit in very well with all those tough biker women. Moreover, she wasn't really up for spending time among a big crowd of rowdy rebels. Her idea of cutting loose was clubbing in a hot nightspot like the one she and Rush danced at in Austin.

A night to remember. She sighed.

* * * Rebar laid in the grass outside Moss's home. He missed the solitude of his Denver lodge yet understood that he needed to stay with his new family until the situation with Malika and Camille was resolved. Besides, getting to know Moss and Levi was important. Chamber staying with them made it feel more like home. They'd been lounging about for a week, taking a break from the intense drama left behind in Amarillo.

He wondered what Cameo was doing or if she'd decided on where to live. His thoughts, though well-trained, refused to accept she'd moved on. His only respite was working on *Face Palm* and other projects, while the guys were at their day jobs. Except for Chamber, who never stayed in one place too long. He continually moved between jobs and at times he seemed a bit lost since they'd quit working on Shade's oil rigs.

"How's the invention coming along?" Chamber plopped down beside him.

"Well...so far I've managed to stabilize Face Palm to stay active for seven days in a host. I've been working on formulas to improve stability and durability."

Chamber leaned over and peeked at Rebar's computer. "Geez, doesn't your brain get tired?"

Rebar laughed. "Nah. I need to keep it busy."

"What's all that scribble?"

"Calculus, equations, physics, chemistry, sets of codes...you know, stuff to solve problems."

"Too bad we can't use numbers and symbols to solve women troubles, eh mate?" Chamber nudged him teasingly.

"I wish." Rebar closed his laptop and took a mental breather.

"Still thinking about...Camille...Cameo?"

"Yeah. I go from wondering if I still have a shot with Cameo to trying to figure out what Camille will pull next."

"How do you like Dallas?"

"Meh." Rebar shrugged. "I miss Denver. Miss my lodge. But it's probably healthier and safer for me to stay here, especially if I want to get past probie status." He laughed a little. "Where do Levi and Moss work? Do they both own this house? What's the deal with them? I haven't seen any women stop by."

"They're not a couple, if that's what you're thinking. Moss owns this place. Levi only stays when something's going on with Ricochet. During tough missions such as this one, they keep their girlfriends away to protect them, if of course they're in a relationship. As you saw, anything can happen."

"Yeah. That was crazy. Where does Levi live?"

"He's got a mobile home about thirty miles north of here, another reason he usually spends summers with Moss. No cover in a mobile home during tornado season."

"Ah, good point. Where do they work?"

"They co-own a moving and storage company. In fact, I think that's the company Rush recommended Cameo for her move. He wanted to make sure her belongings made it down safely."

Rebar felt a wave of remorse and sadness over his foolish loss. "I take it you've talked to him?"

"Who? Rush? Yeah. I check in with him daily for updates."

"What are you doing with yourself since we quit working for Shade? Are you getting restless?"

"I've been helping with Moss and Levi's company, dispatching from their house." Chamber shrugged casually. "You know me. I thrive on change."

"You're incredibly resilient for the lifestyle you live."

"I'll take that as a compliment," Chamber teased.

"Don't you want a permanent relationship? A family? Kids?"

"Not sure. Never thought about kids. I'm heading into my mid-forties. Maybe if the right woman comes along I'll settle down," Chamber replied.

"Had your eyes on Cameo, huh?" Rebar raised a brow.

"Do you blame me? You kicked her to the curb. She's a stone-cold fox and kickass to boot. Not to mention witty and unique."

"So you did have designs on her."

"Rush beat me to it. I still can't figure out how they hooked up so fast." Chamber rubbed his chin in thought.

"Maybe during the fallout in Raton. Nothing brings two people closer than relying on each other for survival. That's how Shade and Camille hooked up. But that was quite a different scenario. Cameo's an angel. She never did anything underhanded like her sister. She's just herself everywhere she goes. No whining. No manipulation. And you're right, she really is kickass. She took Missy and Joan down with surprising ease. I never thought a skinny thing like her could fight." Rebar thought back to that day he and Cameo drove down to Santa Fe. He had it all, then threw it away. "Damn. I sure blew it."

"Stop beating yourself up over it. She's not married or even engaged to another guy yet. Cameo's a smart lady and not likely to jump into a solid commitment too fast."

"Are you saying I may still have a chance with her?"

Chamber gave him a friendly pat on the back. "I don't wanna plant false hope. I'm just advising you, as your friend, to man up a bit and focus on solidifying your position in Ricochet."

"I hear ya." Rebar scoffed with a light laugh. "One of your tough love talks, huh?"

"Yep. Ain't no room in Ricochet for crying in your beer."

Rebar could always count on Chamber to shoot straight. He appreciated the honesty.

"I'll take a cold beer if you're offering," a familiar voice said from behind.

Rebar and Chamber leapt to their feet and spun around to face the unexpected intruder.

"You gotta lotta nerve showing your face here," Rebar said through clenched teeth.

"What's wrong...mate? Missing your gal?" Shade taunted.

"Rebar, don't!" But Chamber's words fell to the ground as Rebar lunged forward.

Shade sidestepped him. "Oh, please." He let out a mocking

laugh. "You really think you can take me on?"

Without a word, Rebar used a leg-sweep move to send the bulked-up prick crashing down hard. Chamber moved forward to help.

"Don't!" he shot back at Chamber. "This is my fight."

Chamber gave a respectful nod and backed off.

"Get up!" Rebar growled at Shade lying on the grass. "Get your ass up and fight like a man."

Shade rubbed the back of his head while pushing to his feet. "I'll tear you limb from limb, boy."

"Go for it," Rebar said in a tone that held no fear.

Shade threw a punch. Rebar ducked then slammed the heel of his hand into Shade's nose. Blood spurted down his chin.

Rage consumed Rebar. He hadn't felt this level of crazed adrenaline since ambushed by the terrorists during the war. From the day of his discharge, he'd silently vowed no man would corner him again.

Shade came at him again, eyes blazing with hate. Rebar spun and delivered a solid kick to his gut. Shade grunted and hunched forward, clearly taken off guard by Rebar's Martial Arts skills.

"Have you forgotten I hold a Black Belt?" Rebar scoffed. Though the encounter had been a surprise, it wasn't unexpected, and Rebar was never off guard. "Are you really that stupid to come here and challenge me?"

Shade looked up slowly. "I didn't come to fight. I want answers, dammit. I know you had something to do with outing the General. How'd you find him? Nobody's ever been able to find him."

"You really need to get over that. The man's dead." Rebar pounced at him, swinging wildly, landing punch after punch into the man's face.

Chamber tried pulling him off. "You're out of control, man. You're gonna kill him!"

Rebar shoved Chamber back and continued pummeling Shade into submission. They rolled a few times on the grass. Shade got a few strikes in, clouting Rebar's eye and chin. He barely felt the pain. Something inside had snapped. He flipped out from under his bulky rival and sprang to his feet. Just as Shade was struggling to get up, Rebar kicked him again, sending him back down. His head bounced off the ground.

Rebar didn't stop. He used every move in his physical arsenal to clobber the guy who'd come between him and Cameo. Kick upon kick. Jab after jab. He couldn't—wouldn't stop until the man lay unconscious or crawled away.

He was barely out of breath by the time Shade lay utterly defeated in a heap on the front lawn. Once certain that Shade was no longer a threat, Rebar stood over him and glared down at his bloodied face.

"I've waited a long time to put you in your place," Rebar seethed, his arms and legs tense, primed to strike again if necessary. "I don't care how big and bad you are. If you ever send that wench to my home again, if you ever interfere in my life again—" He paused to take a breath. "I won't let you off this easy. I'll take you out for good. You came here demanding answers. There's your answer."

Chamber inched closer and laid a hand on Rebar's shoulder. He stared down at Shade, who didn't look so big now. "I'd listen to him...mate. Now get the hell out of here and take that answer back to your pathetic little troop. Or I'll let him kill you."

Shade winced as he touched his bleeding lip, glaring up at them. "You're both insane."

Just then, Moss and Levi pulled up on their Harleys. They parked quickly and rushed to the scene.

"What the hell's going on?" Moss looked from one to another.

"Just giving this prick the answers he came for," Rebar snarled with heavy sarcasm. "He was about to leave, isn't that right, Shade?"

Moss reached under his riding jacket for his firearm. "I don't like troublemakers coming to my home. You're not welcome here. Neither is your slutty fiancée. She's caused enough trouble for my man, here."

Levi arched his brows and laughed. "This is big bad Shade?"

"Yep," Chamber replied.

"Damn. And here I thought we had reason to worry." Levi glanced at Rebar with a slight smirk. "A little angry today?"

"Just a little. Sorry about a scene in your front yard." Rebar stepped away.

"Ah, hell," Moss chuckled. "Not the first time. C'mon, Shade, get your ass up and outta my yard."

Shade staggered to his feet with a groan. Moss shoved him along with the gun at his back.

"I wouldn't incite trouble with Ricochet if I were you," Moss warned. "Wouldn't bode well for you. Got it?"

"Yeah...whatever," Shade mumbled while stumbling along. He shot Rebar a heated glance. "This isn't over yet, bro."

"Hey, I've got more," Rebar started after him again, but Chamber and Levi held him back. "You know where to find me anytime you need another ass-kicking!"

"C'mon, buddy," Chamber said. "I don't need you spiraling. Let's go have a beer."

Rebar sucked in a few calming breaths while watching Moss usher Shade off the property. "That son of a bitch. Can't believe he showed up here demanding answers after what he did. I'll kill him, man. If he comes back, I will."

"You know what, let's skip the beers and take a ride in your Gran Sport," Chamber suggested. "You're wound way too tight."

"Is he gonna be okay?" asked Levi, sounding genuinely concerned.

Chamber nodded. "Long story. PTSD from the war. I got this. Tell Moss thanks and we'll be back in a while."

"Gotcha." Levi gave Rebar a friendly pat on the back. "Nice work, dude. See you guys in a bit."

CHAPTER THREE

Cameo waited on the passenger seat of Rush's Harley while he refueled. They'd been on the road for almost seven hours before a tornadic storm forced them to seek shelter for the night in Lincoln, Kansas, not too far from the Nebraska border. They were almost halfway to Pine Ridge.

"How are you holding up?" Shook asked her while Rush went into the store with Rider and Stoke for beverages.

"Okay." She stared off into the distance, unable to shake a deep sense of sadness that had been creeping over her the past hour.

"What's wrong?" he pressed.

"Nothing." She shrugged.

"Uh-huh." He raised a skeptical brow. "I haven't known you that long, but I sense something."

She sighed. "I can't explain it. I just feel suddenly sad and don't know why."

"Road lag," he said. "A good night's sleep will shake it." He searched her eyes for a few intense moments. "She's hard to forget, isn't she?"

"Who?"

"Malika."

"I'm surprised you're not flipping mad that she used Ricochet to take out the General and his other daughter."

Shook smiled that easy smile of his. "Sometimes I'm so deep undercover, the lines blur," he admitted. "They were hardened criminals."

"So is she," Cameo reminded him.

"Is she, babe?" He gave her a probing look. "Or is she running scared?"

"Better not let Rush hear you say that."

Shook didn't seem fazed. "I have no secrets from him. Malika was a victim of atrocious crimes. I'll find her. Don't worry."

Cameo gasped at the unexpected revelation. "She *did* get to you, didn't she?"

"Is that what her blue feather told you?" he asked with a sly grin.

Her eyes widened. She didn't know what to say. Her hand automatically went to her inner coat pocket to check on the unusual gift—the only tangible proof that Malika's visit wasn't a delusional flashback.

He leaned close and murmured in her ear. "Be careful about hasty judgments."

"H-how did you know?" Goosebumps trickled up her arms.

"Honestly, I don't know. Something odd is going on...spiritually. I'm hoping White Wolf can discern what Malika is or has initiated."

"Please don't tell Rush," she implored.

"I won't. He's not Lakota. He'd only feel threatened by the connection we now share."

"Do you think the way Malika painted her face has anything to do with the way you painted yours?" The question had been burning inside since the encounter.

"Good question, one we'll save for White Wolf. We probably won't even have to ask him. His wisdom has always astounded me."

Rush and the others came out of the store. Cameo zipped her jacket and tried to appear undisturbed by Shook's insight. Rush's gaze shifted between her and Shook but he said nothing. He gave her a sweet kiss then straddled the front seat.

"We're only five minutes from the nearest hotel, angel. Hang in there. You must be exhausted."

"Kinda. Yeah." She glanced at the sky. "Glad we found a place."

Thunder rumbled. Winds coming off the western plains strengthened. Lightning veined across the sky. The storm was gaining on them.

She thought about Rebar tucked safely inside Moss's Dallas home and wondered how he was doing. There were fleeting moments when she missed the coziness of his lodge, his safe haven from the world—the loft. She missed his special Ramen dish and his gentle nature. At times, she worried that she'd moved in with Rush too soon.

But Rush was very persuasive with strong leadership qualities. He didn't take no for an answer lightly. Perhaps a man like him was exactly what she needed. He knew what he wanted and went for it. He worked hard, owned an incredible ranch, a collection of hot cars and an impressive Harley. And on top of that, he was dangerously handsome, undeniably sexy, and stable.

He was in a word—perfection—as far as men go. No emotional baggage. No lingering feelings for another woman. Socially well-rounded with a fabulous circle of friends. She couldn't think of a single flaw that could ruin a relationship.

Yet her heart still carried something for Rebar that she couldn't grasp. Wasn't he all of those things, too? Except for his emotional baggage. Shade, Camille, and Malika ruined everything. Why would her mother align with Shade and use Camille to manipulate Rebar? Even worse, why would her own sister agree to such an evil scheme?

Cameo blamed Shade. His anger and loyalty to the General and determination to uncover Rebar's secrets lowered him to the vilest type of man. In her eyes, Shade was no better than the General.

She felt sorry that Rebar had such an uncaring brother, but she was glad he had severed ties with him. And he did it for her — walked away from the only family he'd ever known, out of loyalty to her. Then he jumped right into the fray to help rescue Malika without ever judging.

Rebar upended his peaceful life because of his love for me.

They'd still be together if not for Camille. If her twin had exhibited a shred of decency, she'd never have agreed to seduce Rebar in an attempt to gain access to his private files.

Then again, Rebar carried his share of blame. He could've resisted Camille, told her no, sent her packing. She wondered if Rebar had been honest about not taking Camille to the Loft.

No. He wouldn't lie.

He'd never been dishonest. And the way he'd set Camille straight in Amarillo, impressed her. In fact, it was that particular standoff that caused her feelings to war.

Ugh. The madness of it all. She wished she could simply turn her feelings off and move on, but this peculiar sorrow in her soul refused to let her go. And why her thoughts kept rebounding to Rebar, frustrated her.

Could she judge him for falling prey to Camille after she herself had fallen into Rush's arms in Santa Fe? *No.* The only difference was that Rebar and Camille's fling had gone public, while nobody knew that in fact, Cameo had passionately kissed Rush in their weak moment before Rebar caved to her twin's deceit.

Even so, she had planned to forget what happened with Rush because of her love for Rebar. She'd have never broken up with Rebar over one night of vulnerability. She thought they were truly in love.

Maybe Shook is right. Maybe I just need sleep.

They arrived at a mediocre motel. The guys secured the bikes, and everyone hurried in to escape the storm. Fortunately, the motel had two rooms facing the parking lot, so she and Rush took one while Rider and Stoke occupied the other.

After she and Rush took turns in the shower, they laid on the bed. It wasn't the nicest bed she'd ever seen but she'd slept on worse.

"What's on your mind tonight, angel?" he asked as they lay facing each other. "You seem down."

"A lot on my mind," she replied.

"Such as?"

"Malika's visit for one. Why on earth was she dressed that way? I swear I'll never understand her."

Rush reached over and took her hand. "You're troubled by more than your mother tonight. You can talk to me. Remember what I said when we first started dating? I know you're rebounding. Keeping your feelings bottled up will confuse you, stress you."

"I do feel sad over Rebar tonight. Not sure why. I haven't been thinking about him that much. It's strange. Over the past hour, I felt this sudden sadness concerning him. I hope he's okay."

"You still care for him." Worry creased his brow.

"I kissed you...more than once in Santa Fe, before he broke up with me. Before Camille seduced him. He still doesn't know that."

"What we did was seek comfort to cope with the dire situation we were in. Don't forget, it was just a few kisses. What Camille did was calculating and wicked. I'm not judging Rebar for losing control. But he broke things off with you. Were you planning to break up with him to be with me?"

She shook her head. "I couldn't do that. Like you said, you and I didn't set out to fall into each other's arms. We weren't even in our right minds."

"Can you forgive him for dumping you cold? Right in front of Camille and Malika?" Rush brushed stray hairs off her face.

"I can forgive him. But not sure I'd be able to trust that it wouldn't happen again," she said.

"Is there more weighing on your mind?"

She sighed, not wanting to burden him.

"Tell me, doll. I won't get upset. You need someone to talk to."

"Just silly things." She slid closer and snuggled against his bare chest. "Like his special Ramen noodles he'd make for me. The lodge...little things. Escaping to his loft was like escaping from everything, even if for a little while."

"Ah, I see. You're missing his home. Didn't you have a sweet little loft apartment? I think Chamber mentioned it."

"Yeah. I loved it." She traced the lines of his chest with one finger while remembering her charming residence. "I loved sitting on the window seat and watching it rain or snow, or just listening to the night sounds, gazing at the moon."

"And Rebar's home gave you that same feeling of escapism."

"I'm sorry. Your home is amazing. I don't mean to sound ungrateful." She felt guilty.

"Nah. Don't worry. I get it." He kissed the top of her head. "I can't cook like Rebar, but I think I can remedy the other situation if you give me a little time." He lifted her chin with a gentle touch so that their eyes met. "Can you do that for me, sugar? Give me a chance to make you feel at home?"

"Yes. You're sweet." She paused then added nervously. "Can I tell you something else?"

"Of course."

"I really can't handle any more steak. I'm afraid to say so though because your friends might think I'm a priss."

He laughed softly. "Aw, babydoll. Why didn't you say something? Maybe I've been trying too hard to impress you. We don't have to eat meat every day. We can have pizza, or subs, or even salad."

"But the guys love your steaks. I don't want to cramp your style."

"Let me tell you something," he said. "Those men adore you and they're your friends...your family now, too. You're the first lady we've ever actually had living within the ranks. Give them a chance to adjust, too. We're probably all tossing out a bit too much testosterone trying to impress you."

"Impress me? My goodness. I'm already beyond impressed. I just don't want to be in the way."

"Ohhh, I see the problem. It was just you and Rebar up in Denver. He was a loner and the two of you hid out in his lodge, away from everyone. You're having trouble getting used to being part of a fulltime family, aren't you?"

She gazed back into his eyes, amazed by his perception. "Yes. I've never had a family. I had work colleagues, but I'd go home alone. I've never had people around twenty-four-seven."

He tapped the tip of her nose playfully. "Don't ya think it's time to give it a try? Unless you prefer living alone."

"No. I've always dreamed of having a family. When Malika found me, then told me I had a twin, I was excited. Couldn't wait to meet her and become part of her life. I made a few attempts to get together for dinner with her family, but she shut me out cold for reasons I may never understand. Then Malika went off the deep end." She brushed his cheek with the back of one hand, admiring his strength and compassion. "Just never thought my family would be all men," she added with a little laugh.

"You'll meet some of the ladies if you hang around long enough. They all have girlfriends, some of them steady, except Shook. His job is demanding. Oh, and Chamber, he has several gals. But that's his business. He rarely brings them around."

She slipped her hand back into his, lacing their fingers together. "Are you sure you still want to take a chance on me? I'm not entirely over what happened, as you just learned."

"I know. You didn't tell me anything I didn't know. I was aware of this when I chose to get involved with you." He lifted her hand to his lips and kissed her fingertips. "Not a doubt in my mind. I'm solid, babe. You'll see."

* * * Rebar kept his eyes on the road as he and Chamber sped down empty highways long after dark. They'd cruised through a drive-through for a quick meal at Chamber's insistence before taking his car out to unwind. He was grateful that his friend still had his back in times of crisis.

"Ya know," Chamber began from the passenger seat. "Might have been helpful to know why Shade drove all the way down to Texas to pay us a visit. I've seen you go through dark times but never saw you go ballistic."

"He wanted answers."

"But why? Seems there was more behind his visit than something he could've asked over the phone."

"He took Cameo from me." Rebar veered into the right lane to pass a slower moving car. "I just snapped when I saw him. I don't know what he expected to find by coming down here. You'd think he'd get that I left for obvious reasons."

"That's why it would've been good to find out what the man is up to. Did you ever consider he came in peace?"

"Hell, no." Rebar scoffed. "Shade doesn't do peace."

Chamber sighed. "I have a feeling we haven't seen the last of him. Something strange is going down. I can feel it."

Rebar shifted gears to pick up speed. "Probably. Maybe he intended to warn us off. No doubt he heard about the General and Missy by now. I don't imagine the news sat well with him. I never did understand why he was so loyal to a man he'd never seen. I just blindly went along with him and all those assignments. It was more than a good paycheck and none of the others seemed to question it either."

"Maybe they know something we don't," Chamber

suggested.

"Like what?" Rebar furrowed his brows. "I don't think Shade has some deep dark secret he's trying to hide. His family dirt hit the floor during the Louisiana ordeal. Doesn't get much worse than finding out his mother was Malika's cohort, and his other brother was conspiring to take over his company."

"Are you bothered that Dale was his full brother and you're only half related? Do you think that contributed to the distance between you and Shade?" Chamber asked. "After all, you were in love with his woman."

"But I never made a move on her. I kept my feelings hidden out of respect for Shade and our father." Rebar pondered that a moment then added, "Not sure why I was so noble about it. Not like our dad didn't bend the rules. He was filthy rich and left his wife home while he traipsed all over the world having affairs. For all I know, there could be more of his bastard sons out there who have never met their father. Maybe even don't know about him."

"True. But it seemed Tassos went out of his way to share the wealth with his sons he knew of. He seemed like a good man with an eye for the ladies," Chamber pointed out.

Rebar laughed. "Coming from one who knows?"

"Hey!" Chamber laughed. "What can I say? I love women. And if any of them come back to tell me I've got a kid, I'll damn well take care of them."

"You better get a steady job then," Rebar teased.

Chamber laughed again, only a bit softer this time. "I wouldn't mind a little Greek son, an Asian daughter, or Native American twins."

"Damn, Chamber. Where all do you go?"

"I love to travel."

"Obviously. And it's nice to see you're all inclusive."

"Never," Chamber said. "A beautiful woman with a caring

heart is a treasure to hold, love, and admire. I always treat them with the utmost respect. I just can't settle on one."

Rebar chuckled. "Thinking of starting a harem?"

"I wish." Chamber leaned back and stretched, then folded both arms behind his head. "I can easily envision that. Stunning ladies lounging around my mansion...or in my case a tent, dressed in their native attire, eating fruit, and feeding me grapes."

"A tent, huh?" Rebar couldn't stop laughing.

"Well, you know, like in Biblical times. Didn't the wealthy sheiks have tents full of women? Lovely nymphs tending the flock, picking dates, dancing in those colorful sheer veils?"

"You're a riot." Rebar turned right toward an exit. "I gotta pull over. I'm laughing too hard. Besides, I need to find some weeds before I piss my pants."

Chamber broke into hearty laughter. Rebar joined him. It felt so great to laugh. They hadn't done this in months, cut loose and enjoy some guy time. Women seemed to think they were the only ones who needed bonding with their friends. He wondered if they ever considered the value men placed on their own friendships, too.

"Ya know," Rebar began once they'd stopped laughing. "I'd be the happiest man in the world with just one woman in my tent, or in my case a lodge. I'm starting to sound like an Indian. But seriously, I was so happy with her. How'd it all fall apart in the blink of an eye?"

Chamber gave him a friendly slap on the back. "I tried to warn you off Camille, mate. Sometimes, we gotta learn the hard way. Cameo isn't even close to walking up the aisle with Rush. Have faith, my friend, have faith. You're one of the most upright guys I know. Tap into your faith and maybe seek spiritual guidance on this one. I think this mountain is beyond my capability to move."

"Good advice." Rebar leaned over and reached into his

glovebox. "I've been neglecting my prayer life. Thanks for the reminder. Let me show you something." He pulled out a small worn box and opened it.

"Watch ya got there?" Chamber leaned in to see.

"A gift from my mom, well, actually from my dad. She gave it to me on my tenth birthday. She said Dad wanted me to have something that would always remind me of him and our faith. For a man who got around, he sounded senti-mental." He lifted a solid gold chain and cross pendant from the box.

"I've never seen you wear it," Chamber noted.

"Nope. Wasn't sure how I felt about Dad. But I kept it safe all these years because it's a gift from my mom who I loved dearly. I wish she were here to meet...never mind, she'd be mortified over what I've done."

"Hey," Chamber softly rebuked. "She'd understand. Maybe she's talking to your heart right now."

Rebar clasped the hook behind his neck and adjusted the cross at his chest. "Time to find my faith again."

"Ya know, Rush has the exact same neckpiece. He never takes it off," Chamber remarked.

"Are you sure it's the same? There are thousands of these kinds of necklaces out there."

Chamber leaned closer. "Sure does look identical to his. Has the same engravings on the cross. Strange."

Rebar shot him a quirky look. "Coincidence."

"Is it valuable?"

"I don't know." Rebar shrugged. "It's eighteen karat gold. I suppose it has some monetary value. It's over forty years old. She said Tassos gave it to her at my birth for her to keep for me."

"He does sound like a sentimental guy."

Rebar tried to recall seeing a neck-chain on Rush but eve-rything from those few days was a blur and he typically didn't pay much attention to how other guys dressed unless it jumped out at him. He shrugged it off. No way could they have the exact same necklace.

"I used to feel a little judgmental toward my father for having the affair. Even so, I admired how he cared for Mom. Now that I've experienced how easy it is to muck things up, I definitely don't have room to fault my dad. Whatever he struggled with is between him and his Maker. I'll never judge anyone again. I'm more on a quest for forgiveness," Rebar said, opening up more than usual to his friend.

"For everyone or just a certain lady?"

Rebar furrowed his brows, slighted by the insinuation. "You know me. I don't hold a grudge. Someday, I'll probably even forget what Shade did. But yeah, I'm not giving up on Cameo." He opened his car door. "Be right back." As he stood off the berm in the darkness of night relieving his bladder, he noticed lightning zigzagging in the far distance to the north. The skies looked ominous even in the dark. Each flash of light revealed heavy thunderheads. He zipped his fly and jumped back in the car. "We should get back. Looks like serious weather headed our way. Clouds are moving south.

Chamber peered out the window. "Yep. Get this thing in gear, man. I'm not a fan of tornados."

"I've never seen one but can't say I want to." Rebar revved his Stage One engine and turned the car back toward Denton County where Moss lived.

A large piece of metal tumbled across the road, barely missing them. Suddenly the wind began to roar.

"Whoa! Debris!" Chamber shouted. "We're in trouble."

"Hold on!" Rebar tromped the gas pedal. "There's nowhere to shelter around here. We're gonna have to outrun it."

CHAPTER FOUR

"Rebar!" Cameo bolted upright in bed. Cold sweat beaded her bare arms and legs. She panted heavily.

Rush woke with a start from a sound sleep. "Halo, what's wrong?"

Her gaze darted around the small room. Lightning flashed outside the window easily visible through the drapes. A crack of thunder made her jump. Wind groaned against the walls and whistled around the eaves.

"It's just a storm, baby." He pulled her into a comforting embrace. "Just a storm."

Her thoughts ran wild. She couldn't tell him that she had a nightmare involving Rebar. At least that's what she thought it was. *Or did I have a premonition?* She sensed Rebar was hurting and in serious danger. Tears filled her eyes. She was glad for the cover of night so Rush couldn't see her face.

Rebar...where are you? She felt his fear, his rage, his pain. At this very moment, she missed him so much. She wished they were safe in the loft enjoying a favorite movie or snack. She began to realize she should've rented out her own apartment in Austin as planned instead of moving in with Rush. But he was hard to resist and moving to a new locale on her own felt scary with all that was happening in her life.

"I can't sleep during storms," she muttered against Rush's chest.

"No worries. We can watch TV or talk."

She eased from his arms and went to the window and pulled the drapes aside. "It looks nasty out. Does this place

34

have a basement?"

"Probably not. Don't worry, most of these storms blow right by."

"Yeah, but what do they take with them?" She cast him a worried look.

A smile touched his lips. "We'll be fine, doll. I haven't seen Dorothy's house fly by yet," he teased.

"Ha-ha, wise guy." She wrapped her arms tight around her, hugging herself while saying a silent prayer.

Please, Lord, protect us and watch over Rebar.

A trashcan blowing by the window startled her. She squeezed her eyes shut and prayed again. She didn't understand how she could feel Rebar's pain or sense peril around him. She asked God to help him and bless him. She no longer felt angry over his bad decision but instead a sense of compassion filled her heart regarding him.

"Angel, come back to bed," Rush softly called. "Come dawn, we have another long ride ahead of us."

She went to the bed and crawled under the sheets. Rush wrapped muscled arms around her and kissed her cheek. She focused on his calm rhythmic breathing instead of the violent weather slamming the motel. Remembering the feather, she reached into her jacket hanging on the bedpost and wrapped her fingers around the soft plume.

Whether it was Lakota Medicine or peace from God, her nerves calmed, and she began to feel drowsy.

The hush of dawn ushered in clear skies and slightly cooler weather on the first day of August. Cameo loved the brief period between sunrise and moonset, where no shadows were cast, night creatures had quieted, and birds had not yet woken with song.

Perfect peace. Perfect silence.

She'd been back in America for three months now. Memories of her first week in the States drifted through Cameo's mind as she lay waiting for Rush to wake.

She thought about the day Rebar chased her down, then begged her for a date, writing her number on his hand and their first night at his lodge. He'd slammed on the brakes when their mutual attraction took off too fast. His heart was guarded and so was hers. But they'd talked their way through the barriers and found beautiful love and trust.

She pulled on her clothes and sat at the edge of the bed staring at the feather before Rush woke. She flipped it back and forth by rolling the quill between two fingers. *A feather. That's all my mother left me, a blue feather. She stole my guy, killed four people, and created utter chaos in my life, then leaves me a feather.* She returned the feather to the inside pocket of her jacket.

Shattered dreams.

She sighed, then slid out of bed and walked to the window. Trash, furniture, and miscellaneous debris littered the parking lot. They'd survived a wicked storm. Something brushed the top of her head. She squealed and jumped back, swatting frantically at her hair for fear a spider or large insect landed on her. The room was still somewhat dark.

"You're awake already," Rush said much calmer than she felt.

When she stopped her flurry of panicked movements, she glanced up and saw a webbed ring adorned with feathers hanging from the upper window frame. *A dreamcatcher?* She tilted her head, staring curiously.

"Do you see that?"

"Yeah..." he replied. "Strange. It's possible we didn't notice it with the storm and all. Plus, we were really tired. This *is* Native American territory."

Cameo felt an eerie chill yet at the same time a sense of peace, as if her Lakota roots had protected them from the storm. Either way, she had never understood Native Medicine in any culture and felt somewhat uneasy that it now seemed to be following her.

"I'm ready to hit the road. Can't wait to meet White Wolf. I hope he has some answers."

"Are the bikes still there?" he asked with a wink.

"I don't see them. The parking lot is a wreck. Cars and trash all over the place."

He sprang from the bed and in two steps was at the window. Then he released a heavy sigh of relief. "That was cruel." He narrowed his eyes at her and almost smiled.

"Hm." She laid one finger alongside her cheek and gazed innocently upward. "About as cruel as making me eat that tough and spicy meal at that dive you took me to?"

"Whoa ho, you don't forget a thing, do ya?" He laughed then tickled her into a fit of giggles. "You're a tricky one."

Someone pounding on their door interrupted the light moment.

"Hey," came Stoke's voice from the other side. "Motel management asked us to check out so they can clear the lot."

Rush sighed. "I'll get you later," he said to Cameo, then to Stoke, "All right, we'll be ready in no time."

Cameo quickly gathered her belongings and strolled outside. Streaks of early morning sun glinted off the bikes. The weather was gorgeous. The humidity had dropped significantly and there wasn't a cloud in a clear blue sky. She took a deep breath of morning air, refreshing her soul from a dark night.

Fortunately, the guys had secured their Harleys close to the building. Other than minor scratches and dents, the bikes seemed okay. However, that was from her perspective. She heard them moaning and nearly weeping over their precious babies while closely examining their bikes.

"Well," Shook said with a heavy sigh. "Overall, we got lucky. Look at this parking lot. At least our bikes only incurred cosmetic damage. We can easily fix 'em up when we get back home."

"That's the spirit," Rider added. "Hey, what biker hasn't taken a beating in a storm or two? Those hailstone dents are battle scars well earned."

Stoke chuckled. "We certainly won't look like rookies if any veterans pass us while heading to Sturgis."

"True," Shook agreed with a light laugh. "We're not far from there." He shot Rush a hopeful look.

"No. We're not going," Rush said. "After we visit the Medicine Man, we're going back home."

Cameo walked around the bikes then handed her backpack to Rush. "They look good to me," she said.

"Where's your riding jacket?" Rush asked. "You need protection on long runs."

"Oh, shoot. I left it on the bedpost. I'll be right back." She dashed back into the motel room.

Wow. Can't believe I almost left this behind. She lifted it to her nose and inhaled the scent of leather and fine cologne, then wondered if Rebar had ever noticed his favorite jacket missing. He'd left it at Rush's after his last visit. She hadn't had the chance to return it and with the impromptu road trip, she needed a jacket as hers still smelled funky from the teargas. *Ha! Who am I kidding? I wanted to keep it.* His jacket was one of the few familiar things in her life at the moment.

Something on the floor caught her eye. Looking down, she saw a trail of blue feathers. As if compelled, she followed them into the bathroom. Blue smoke swirled up from the tiles. An icy chill filled the room. Malika appeared out of nowhere, looking just as she had in Rush's kitchen.

"What do you want?" Cameo wrapped her arms around her midriff as if to shield herself from the uninvited presence. She stared guardedly. "Why are you following me? How did you even get here?"

"Cameo, my brave one. Rebar is trapped inside his car

from last night's storm. He's in danger."

"How do you know this?"

"Please trust me this time. It's not a trick. I'm trying to...trying to..." Then she simply vanished and took the smoke with her.

Cameo backed away. Confusion inundated her. She hurried back to the bed and grabbed his jacket then noticed that the dreamcatcher was gone from the window. Feeling freaked out, she ran from the room.

"Where's your fringed jacket?" Rush asked with a peculiar look when she returned to the bike.

"It stinks from the rendezvous in Amarillo." It had taken him this long to notice... She hopped on behind him.

"Isn't that Rebar's?" he pried.

"Yes. He left it behind last week." She didn't mind that it was huge on her. The roomy jacket felt safe, and it smelled like Rebar.

"I see." Rush fired up the engine and led the way as they resumed their trek to South Dakota.

She held onto Rush's waist with one hand and texted Chamber with the other. When he didn't reply, she decided to try Moss. She refrained from contacting Rebar directly for fear of arousing Rush's jealousy. He was already sensing her turmoil. He didn't need to know her every thought.

This is Halo. She tapped send.

A few seconds later Moss replied. *Is everything all right? We had bad storms up here last night. Are you all safe?*

We had them, too. Rebar and Chamber didn't come back last night. They must've hunkered down somewhere.

Rebar's hurt! Please find him.

How do you know? Did he contact you?

No. Just please trust me. I can't explain right now. Find him and let me know.

Will do, Halo. Be safe. By the way, where are you?

We are headed up to Pine Ridge. Explain later.

Got it. TTYS.

She sent a heart emoji and tucked her phone back into her pocket.

* * * "This is not good," Rebar muttered, trying to shift his weight against the steering wheel. "Are you okay over there?" He tried to turn his head and see Chamber. "Hey...wake up."

Chamber groaned. "What happened to outrunning it?"

"My car is fast but apparently not faster than a twister. We got rolled and we're pinned in and hanging."

"We need to get out of here before another one turns this thing into scrap metal," Chamber said, sounding worried but not panicked.

"Hey." Rebar frowned. "You'll hurt her feelings."

"Excuse me if I'm a bit grouchy hanging upside down like a bat," he joked with a tense laugh.

"I think the storms have passed so you can relax. But we are in a predicament." Rebar tried reaching for his phone but couldn't move more than an inch or so.

"How long have we been trapped here?"

"I don't know. We must've blacked out from the hit. Damn. I had the engine gunned. Last thing I remember is seeing something whip past the windshield."

Chamber sighed. "We got rolled for sure. Where are we?"

"Do I look like I can reach my GPS?" He scoffed. "Somewhere outside of Denton County."

"Guess we should've checked the weather before heading out last night."

"Never had to worry much up in Denver," Rebar said. "Not sure how long I'll stay in Texas. I miss my lodge."

"Can't say I blame ya." Chamber sniffed the air. "You smell that?"

Rebar drew a deep breath. "Shit. Gasoline." He managed to glance out the broken window. "Sun's coming up. Blistering Texas heat is gonna bake and burn us for breakfast."

"We need to get outta here, mate." Chamber began struggling against the seatbelt holding him in place. "If I could just reach the buckle." He grunted and squirmed to no avail. "Damn, Rebar...we're in a bind here."

"I don't think there's anyone around. No use wasting our energy hollering for help. Seems the twister threw us way off the main road. I just saw a tumbleweed roll past my window."

"Hey," Chamber muttered. "Maybe now would be a good time to rekindle that prayer life you were talking about before we got rolled."

"Yeah..." Rebar agreed. He realized their situation was a lot worse than either of them let on. He felt fine physically but couldn't tell if Chamber was injured. They needed help and they needed it now. He closed his eyes and took a calming breath. Being pinned and hanging upside down was beginning to mess with his head.

"Hey, mate," Chamber said, concern echoed in his voice. "We'll get out. Stay with me here. Keep your thoughts trained on something positive, okay?"

"Okay." Rebar nodded once and focused on the loveliest thing he could think of—a beautiful angelic face surrounded by a halo of long golden blonde hair. Then he clutched the cross pendant and prayed.

Several minutes later, Chamber interrupted his meditation. "Not trying to hurry you along or anything...but are those flames coming from under the hood?"

Rebar opened his eyes. "Yep."

"Well, my friend," Chamber said sadly. "If we gotta go, at least we're together. I couldn't ask for a better friend with who to make that journey."

"No..." Rebar said. "Not like this." Gunfire rang in his ears. Then the deafening whoosh of a grenade landing in the dirt. He watched fire engulf the front of his car. "Cameo...Halo..." He closed his eyes to block out the horror which had become his life.

Everything went black.

Rebar heard muffled voices.

Loud clanging and a horrid grating noise drew him momentarily from grogginess. He turned his head in slow motion to look at Chamber, who appeared unconscious.

"Hey..." he said in a raspy voice. "Don't you quit on me."

Chamber didn't respond.

A burst of fresh air filled the interior of the car followed by blinding light. He made out silhouettes against the light. They were working frantically to drag Chamber from the car.

Good. My buddy will be saved.

He closed his eyes again and drifted through a void. Without Cameo, his heart felt empty. He didn't care about the car or fighting the war any longer.

"No. Save my buddy," he muttered when multiple hands began dragging him from the wreckage. "I won't leave him behind."

"Rebar, we got him, man. Help us out here. Can you move your legs?" a man asked him.

He nodded and pushed off the floor with his feet.

"Good job, mate. Keep pushing. C'mon! This thing's about to blow."

Rebar summoned what was left of his willpower and shoved his body upward. Hands grabbed his arms and waist then heaved him from the vehicle. He felt his T-shirt rip as his back scraped the road.

Someone shouted, "Get down!"

And two bodies fell on top of him. *Who are they?* His mind flashed back to that ditch. The stench of smoke and burning metal stung his nose. He started yelling profanities, cursing the dirty rebels as they hauled him away from the safety of his tank.

"Is he alive?" Rebar hollered.

"Yeah, man. You're both gonna be okay. Hang in there."

CHAPTER FIVE

They rolled into Pine Ridge at sunset after ten hours on the road through Nebraska. Damage from multiple storms had forced them to detour a few times.

Cameo didn't feel as fatigued as she was from the first jaunt. She seemed to be adapting to motorcycles quickly. Rush, Stoke and Rider looked invigorated from the ride, a clear indicator that biking was their passion.

Rush dropped back to let Shook take the lead. Rider fell in behind her and Rush. She admired how they navigated the roads and traveled as a team.

During their trip, she got to see breathtaking landscapes of America's heartland. Such vast spans of untamed land. She never tired of nature's beauty and felt blessed for having seen so much of it all over the world.

An hour after crossing into South Dakota, they continued northwest for two more hours to the Black Hills. Cameo paid attention to road signs to follow their journey. Taking in the view by motorcycle was incredible. From the Great Plains to more rugged terrain consisting of rolling hills, ravines, and steep flat-topped hills then into the thick cover of evergreens in Black Hills territory, she could picture her ancestors dominating this vast wilderness.

Shook led them along single-lane roads deep into a wooded area, winding and climbing until they pulled into a dirt drive which brought them to a small clearing bearing a lone cabin.

A triangular vertical structure made of what looked like

poles carved from tree branches was erected over a fire pit with the base of the poles stuck in the dirt and the tops bound together. It almost resembled a teepee but without the skins. A thicker branch was inserted horizontally across the center, leading her to suspect it was a makeshift spit.

Upon their approach, an elderly man exited the cabin and stood with straight back, squared shoulders, and a dignified expression on his weathered face.

He must be White Wolf, she thought. He wore buckskin pants and a colorful gauze shirt. Two long white braids hung past his shoulders to his waist with a feather attached to each one, and a beaded headband added an air of nobility.

The guys parked their bikes in a row alongside the cabin and cut the engines. Shook was the first one to dismount and greet the Native American man.

"White Wolf, it is good to see you, my friend." The two men clasped forearms.

White Wolf's black eyes brightened. "Tasunke! Many years have passed since you've come to my lodge. How are you?"

"Tah-sunk-ah?" she repeated softly. "Is that your last name?"

Shook turned those haunting black eyes on her. "It was my only name growing up. I added Shook when I joined the military."

"What does it mean?"

"Horse," he replied.

"Interesting." She looked from him to the Medicine Man, noticing a striking resemblance between the two.

White Wolf made eye contact with her. "You bear the shadow of your ancestors," he said directly.

A tiny gasp escaped her. *Shadow Portrait, the meaning of my name that Mother gave me. How could he tell? I'm so blonde and blue eyes...* She recoiled toward Rush, shocked by this man's insight at first glance.

He smiled a toothless grin then waved them to the fire pit.

"Come, my friends. Let's sit a while. I have not received visitors in a long time."

"Are you okay, angel?" whispered Rush as they found a spot in the circle.

"Just shocked," she replied. "He must be wise, as Shook said."

Rush stroked her hair. "Your Native American heritage seems to be more active lately."

"Ha, ya think?" She scoffed. She hadn't told him about the feather trail or Malika's second visit and wasn't sure she would.

Shook gestured toward each of the guys. "These are some of my friends, my family," he told White Wolf. "Rush, Stoke and Rider. And we call the girl Halo."

The man smiled and nodded while packing a long pipe with tobacco. "Let us share the peace pipe for unity." He took a long drag then passed it to Shook who did the same and passed it on.

"I don't smoke," Cameo said sheepishly.

"Simply take a puff and blow it out," Shook told her. "As a symbol of acceptance. Pretty thing like you shouldn't inhale this stuff anyway."

Gingerly, she wrapped her lips around the wooden tip and sucked in a mouthful of smoke. The tobacco tasted slightly sweet. She let the smoke flow back through her lips and as the last one to take a hit, she handed the intricately carved piece to Shook. He inhaled another drag then exhaled slowly.

White Wolf grinned upon receiving the pipe back. "I have a story for you," he said.

"But we came for answers," Cameo whispered to Shook.

"Sshh," he hushed her. "We'll get to that in his time. For now, we must listen."

"Sorry," she whispered, then sat back and crossed her legs on the grass, feeling embarrassed over her rude impatience.

Shook patted her leg reassuringly. "No worries, babe. I know this is new to you."

White Wolf stared at her with a piercing gaze for several long moments. "I will not bore you, Halo. I've waited many moons to see Tasunke again. I'm old and there are things he must know before I join our ancestors in the spirit world."

"My apologies," she said humbly.

He accepted her apology with a nod then continued speaking. "Long ago, before the Great Spirit gave me my calling, I was a wild young warrior living with the Nation," he told them. "I met a beautiful young maiden when every third moon her family visited the reservation. They brought silk, linen, and jewels to our women in exchange for our handmade flutes. Their daughter and I fell in love. We would sneak off to the river at each visit."

A surprised look sparked in Shook's eyes. "You never told me this story, wise one."

"No, I did not. It was my burden to bear. But now, you are a man, and I will soon cross the great river. I longed to tell you many times. However, the Tribal Council forbade me to speak of it."

"You no longer fear the Council?" Shook asked.

"No. All those who knew of my history are gone. The new generation does not care about tales from an old man."

Enlightenment swept over Shook's face. "She was my mother, wasn't she?"

White Wolf scowled. "You are impatient today."

"I'm sorry." Shook backed down immediately. "Please, say what you need to say."

"The maiden had hair like golden wheat and eyes like rain. Her smile outshined the sun, and her voice was gentle as a dove. I called her Rain Song, though her white name was Olivia. Oh, how we loved each other. I lived for those visits. Then one time her parents came without her. They refused to speak with me." White Wolf let out a heavy sigh. "Months went by with no news about Rain Song. Every third moon, I waited. She didn't come. Twelve moons passed before I saw her again. On her last visit, Rain Song arrived with an infant at her breast. I thought she'd married and that was why her parents kept her away. That was the last time her family traded with our people, and the last time I saw my love. I stood a few feet away as she, with tears in her eyes, handed her baby to the Chief. I couldn't hear what was said but I understood their faces."

"You never saw her again?" Cameo asked, dabbing tears from her eyes at his sad tale.

He shook his head. "The Tribal Council held a meeting that night and decided that the infant would be nursed by the Chief's youngest wife as she had recently birthed a child. Once the babe was weaned, I was asked to leave the reservation and take my son with me because I had shamed my people."

Shook stood, visibly shaken with emotion, and walked to White Wolf. "Thank you for telling me. I always sensed that you were my father but didn't dare disrespect you by asking."

White Wolf rose to his feet, trembling slightly. "My son. I'm proud of who you've become. I see honor in your soul, strength in your spirit and Rain Song's gentleness in your heart. I'm sorry I never told you before now. I have prayed every day that the Great Spirit would bring you to me before I leave this world. And now my prayer is answered, and my soul is at peace. Your mother had no choice. Neither of us did. We were young and in love. Our elders decided for us what would be."

"My mother...is she still alive?" Shook asked.

"I do not know. I'm sorry you never knew her, but it was probably for the best. She married a wealthy businessman and never looked back. I chose the path of Medicine Man to redeem the disgrace I brought to our Tribe."

"You bear no shame, Father," Shook hugged him. "There is no shame in love, only in prejudice."

White Wolf clung to Shook with intense emotion. Cameo whisked tears from her cheeks. Never did she expect that Shook would find his real father and learn about his birth-mother on this journey. She felt happy for him, though the story was sorrowful, at least he had half a happy conclusion.

"My son..." White Wolf pulled back and placed both hands firmly on Shook's shoulders. Pride beamed on his wrinkled face. "Now, my son...what can I do for you?"

"That's it?" Cameo questioned with lifted brows. "After fifty years you receive the truth about your parents and that's all the emotion you have to share?"

White Wolf laughed. "Halo does not yet understand the Lakota way."

"We're men, babe," Shook told her. "Emotions are for women to show and men to learn from. We celebrate our feel-ings in other ways such as eating and smoking around a good fire." He took another drag from the pipe and passed it to Rush.

"And dancing," White Wolf added. "Tonight, we'll roast meat over a big fire and dance to the drums of our ancestors. A great truth has been revealed. A great burden has been lifted. We celebrate as men...as warriors."

"Oh." She sat back on her knees, staring at them curiously.

Two men had just reunited as father and son after decades apart and their reaction was totally...male. Then again, maybe it was more than male, maybe it truly was Lakota because her mother hadn't expressed much emotion upon their reunion either.

The thought of more meat dimmed her appetite. A sup-posed fifteen-hour trip had turned into twenty. Her butt and legs were sore, her stomach growled, and her body was sweaty, yet she uttered no complaint. Now they were going to eat White Wolf's food. Only God knew what White Wolf was going to cook over the crude fire. She began to regret asking Shook to lead them here.

Nevertheless, here she was, far from home. On the upside, Shook gained a true blessing to learn that he'd been raised by his actual father and to hear the touching, albeit sad love story of his parents.

White Wolf walked into his cabin without a word.

"Did I offend him?" Cameo worried.

"Nah." Shook laughed a little. "He went in to get the meat. We should build the fire. It will be good to share a fire with him, knowing he's my father."

"I'm happy for you. But when can we ask him about Malika?"

"We won't need to. He'll tell us what he knows when he's ready," Shook told her.

"How does he know what we want?"

"He recognized you right away. I'm sure he's already pondering your presence here. His medicine is from the old ways, powerful. You'll see." Shook gave her a wink.

She took a breath and sighed. Rush, Rider, and Stoke had been unusually quiet. Then again, they looked completely stoned from smoking whatever White Wolf passed around. The smoke didn't smell like any ordinary tobacco she'd smelled. She had a pretty good idea of what they'd smoked.

Great. I'm in the middle of nowhere with four bikers and an ancient Medicine Man, and they're all high as a kite.

White Wolf returned carrying a huge bird, already plucked. "I trapped this last night. Your timing is good. The bird is drained of blood and ready to cook." He grinned at Halo as if sensing her repulsion. "Got a lot of big feathers from it, too."

"What is it?" she whispered to Shook, who seemed the least high.

"Wild turkey," he replied. "Turkey feathers are highly sought after by Native Americans. They are used in many ways by our people. Didn't Malika tell you anything about your heritage?"

"Not much. I've only had about two conversations with her since we met, hardly had time to discuss Native heritage. Are we really going to eat that thing?" She cringed slightly.

"Hell, yeah. You've never tasted anything like wild turkey over a fire." Shook squeezed her hand. "Relax, babe. Maybe you should've inhaled some of that pipe."

She sat back and watched the men build a robust fire in the pit while White Wolf tressed the turkey then tied it to the spit. He sat on a large rock and turned the stick every fifteen minutes or so.

Rider and Stoke were making small talk, joking around about ghosts and just being ridiculously silly. Rush seemed pensive and withdrawn. She scooted over to his side when he sat back down.

"Is everything okay?" she asked him.

"Yeah," he replied softly. "Just feeling rather strange. Wish I hadn't smoked that shit. I've never been into it."

"Are you getting paranoid?" She studied his face.

"A little. You have a lot in common with Shook. You're wearing Rebar's jacket. Where do I fit in here tonight, angel?"

"How do you think I feel? I'm the only one not stoned."

He raked a hand through his hair. "Sorry. Whatever he put in that pipe had a hell of a kick."

"Looks like we're camping here then," she muttered. "Well, I hope I at least get answers about Malika and her blue feathers."

White Wolf turned sharply and stared at her. She shrunk beneath his penetrating gaze and thought surely he was about to say something, but he simply turned back toward the fire.

Once the turkey was cooked, the men ate heartily and

drank red wine offered by the old man. She passed on the drink and sipped her bottled water instead. Though wild turkey wasn't on her list of favorite foods, she'd eaten worse, so she nibbled on a section of roasted meat to show respect.

"Now we dance," White Wolf said and began beating a drum while hopping and twirling around the blazing fire.

The men followed suit. Cameo watched intently as the men she thought she knew gyrated like savages to the hypnotic rhythm of the drum. The Medicine Man chanted in Lakota as their dancing grew more feverish.

What on Earth did he put in that pipe? She wondered.

She became drawn to the fire, into their primitive dancing and the chanting. She noticed White Wolf tossing bits of something into the fire. *Feathers!* He was tossing turkey feathers into the flames. The smoke began to turn blue.

What's happening? She curled into a ball, wrapping her arms around both legs while watching in anticipation. Suddenly, an unseen force shoved her from behind, compelling her to join the circle. She felt awkward at first and took tiny steps, made little hops trying to emulate the men.

Then her mood shifted. The beat of the drum felt like part of her, luring her deeper into a trance-like state of mind. The night in Austin flashed through her mind of when she'd danced completely uninhibited. Closing her eyes, Cameo let the drums of her ancestors carry her into their world.

She began leaping and whirling with arms stretched out. She flung her hair back with a toss of her head and spun around as she danced. It was as if she could hear hundreds of drums and singing voices reverberating around her. A hazy smile curved her lips when she felt herself connect with the spirits of her people.

Upon opening her eyes slightly, she gasped in shock. Dancing *with* her was Malika in all her stunning glory—blue and purple face paint, the same white markings on her flawless skin, and brightly colored feathers adorning her headdress. Her sleek black hair flowed freely from its usual braid, swirling around her like an ebony halo.

Her mother reached over and draped a multi-colored, fringed shawl over her daughter's shoulders yet kept hold of each end. They made solid eye contact and danced together around that fire.

Cameo had never seen anything more beautiful than Malika freely dancing with grace, like a doe frolicking through a meadow. Her mother lifted the shawl into the air then manipulated the silky fabric artistically between and around them, as if that sheer stretch of fabric carried years of lost time and she was weaving the broken pieces of their past back together.

Love flowed over Cameo, through her. She embraced it with her soul. Even if this mystical experience was but an illusion, she would carry it in her heart forever because somewhere deep within her spirit she knew a supernatural connection was taking place.

A sudden gust of wind blew between them and just like that, Malika was gone. Blue mist lingered in her place and the shawl laid at Cameo's feet. She scooped it off the ground and held it to her chest. The scent of roses wafted past her nose. Dropping to her knees, she lowered her head and cried, overwhelmed by it all.

"You're the shadow of Feather Blue," came White Wolf's troubling declaration.

"Um. I think you have me mixed up with someone else," Cameo said with all due respect. "I have a twin."

"Yes. But she is not the shadow of her mother. She carries the materialism of her white father. But you, you are one with nature. You speak to animals and care for them. You love Mother Earth and work hard to protect her. You are not the shadow of your sister. You carry your mother's Lakota spirit...and her enchanting way."

She glanced at Shook, then Rush, then back at White Wolf. "How could you know all this? Did one of the guys tell you about me?"

He walked back to his place beside the fire and sat on the ground. "Search your heart. You know that is not possible."

His knowledge fascinated her. She sat beside him. "You summoned her tonight. The feathers you tossed into the fire...were to draw her here, weren't they?"

"Yes. I sensed your aura the moment our eyes met. I had a feeling you were the lost child of Feather Blue."

"Feather Blue," Cameo repeated to herself. *So lovely.* Her eyes widened with interest. "You knew her?"

He nodded. "If my memory serves me right, Feather would be in about her fifty-seventh year now. She was only sixteen when she became pregnant with twins and left the reservation. Nobody ever heard from her again. Her parents left this Earth never knowing what happened to their daughter."

"Oh. How sad."

"I followed her spirit the best I could. Most of the time it was too dark to see. But once in a while I'd catch a glimpse of her. I prayed she'd find her way back."

Cameo sighed. "I'm not sure she did. She seems confused."

"She gave you the blue feather recently, didn't she?" he asked but seemed to already know.

She glanced nervously at Rush. "Yes. She said it's for protection."

White Wolf looked over at Rush then back at her. "She told you the truth but there is more. The blue feather is the essence of her soul. Deep betrayal must've occurred for her to extend herself in such a powerful way."

Cameo looked down. "Yes."

"Feather is still caught in the realm of confusion. Many tales were shared over fires about the Legend of Feather Blue." White Wolf appeared deeply concerned. "She possesses strong magic and uses it to deceive."

"What about the lines she painted on her face. They resemble the lines Shook uses undercover."

White Wolf nodded thoughtfully. "A connection. She's trying to attach her spirit to his."

"She's not declaring war against him?"

"No. White is for peace. She wants something from Shook." He turned toward his son and asked, "You're involved with Feather Blue? How can this be? You're several years younger than she."

"Not involved," Shook clarified. "She's wanted by the law and I'm an undercover FBI Agent. Malika and I spent time together during a sting op. But it didn't go well."

"Hm." White Wolf fired up his pipe again. "I need to pray about her intentions toward you. It is late. We should sleep now." He gathered himself together and went into his cabin without saying anything further.

"Is he angry?" Cameo asked.

"Nope. He needs to meditate," Shook replied, then looked at his friends. "And we need to sleep. You all look wasted," he told them.

"How are you still so damn alert?" asked Rush. "My brain's been in a fog for hours. And the dance...that was intense." He turned his gaze on Cameo. "I saw you dancing with her. I'm still trying to wrap my mind around it."

Stoke and Rider were lying on the grass counting stars, still totally blitzed.

"We should get some sleep," she said. "Hopefully things will look clearer in the morning." She felt Shook staring at her. "Are you worried?" she asked him.

"Me? Nah. I will admit this has been an extraordinary evening. I'll grab the bedrolls from the bikes. Those three are toasted." He laughed a little. "Are you okay?"

"Yeah..." She thought back to when she first learned of her

Lakota heritage during a dinner with Malika, and how she longed to tap into those roots. Never did she imagine it would lead to this.

CHAPTER SIX

Cameo woke early, just as the morning sun filtered through thick pines. Her stomach growled with hunger. She quietly got up and let Rush sleep while she wandered around the campsite. Her hair was a tangled mess. She finger-combed it, tugging grass and dried weeds from within her long tresses.

"What do you seek?" White Wolf whispered as he walked into the clearing from the woods.

"Something to boil water in," she replied.

"Come." He waved for her to follow.

She walked behind him into his humble cabin, almost afraid of what she might see. But to her surprise it wasn't full of animal pelts and deer antlers. On the contrary, his abode presented a strong ambiance of peace. A single cot stood against one wall covered by what looked like a colorful hand-woven blanket. A woodburning stove stood in a corner beside a small sink basin that was tapped into an outside water pump.

"I just pumped fresh water," he told her, then gestured toward a tin coffee pot. "Though I live in the traditional way of my people, I love the white man's coffee." He grinned. "I have not yet brewed a pot this morning, so there is hot water on the stove. Help yourself."

"Thank you very much," she inclined her head and smiled, then poured hot water from a metal saucepan into the foam cup containing her Ramen noodles.

White Wolf watched her with marked interest, then peered into her white cup. "You eat poor man's food?"

57

She shrugged sheepishly. "They are my favorite."

"There is not meat in there," he noted.

"Sure there is," she countered. "See those tiny pink things? They're dried shrimp."

He wrinkled his brows and chuckled. "We rarely see shrimp here. Most of those who live on the reservation make their own food from what we receive. Sometimes, it's not much."

"I am sad that the Nation is not better cared for by the government," she told him.

"Your compassion is admirable." He poured the hot water into the coffee pot then set it on the black iron stove. "I will offer the men coffee. They probably need it." He chuckled again.

She cast him a quizzical smile. "What did you put in that pipe?"

"Ohh, a mix of this and that."

"This and that, huh?" She laughed softly. "More that than this? Shook told me not to inhale."

"My son is wise. He knew I would summon Malika. He wanted you to be alert. The peyote in the cannabis helped your friends accept what they saw."

"You do realize that your son is a Federal Agent, don't you?"

White Wolf nodded. "We are exempt from United States laws, especially our medicines that we use for religious and medicinal purposes. Last night was a ceremonial experience. Tasunke knows our ways. There is no worry."

"I'll wait outside." She gave him a respectful nod then left the cabin and practically collided with Rush.

"Geez!" He blew out a breath. "I was worried about you."

"I'm sorry. I woke up early and needed water. White Wolf has a cute little setup in there," she told him.

"What ya eating?" He glanced at her cup.

"Ramen."

"Where'd you find a cup of noodles out here?"

"I packed some." She smirked. "You told me to pack light."

He gripped his head with both hands. "I'd laugh if I wasn't so hungover."

"Do you remember last night?"

"Somewhat," he replied. "Dancing, strange visions..." He searched her eyes. "You...I saw you dancing around the fire. I was mesmerized."

"Is that all you saw?" She wasn't sure how much the others were supposed to know.

"As far as I can recall. Everything that happened after we smoked up is a blur."

White Wolf appeared with the tin coffee pot and four metal cups. "Are your friends awake yet? Or do they sleep until the sun is high?"

"We're awake," Rush replied. "What do you have there?"

"Black coffee to clear your mind." He wandered over to the fire and sat on his rock. Sunlight shimmered off his white hair.

Rush took Cameo's hand and led her to a spot near the fire-pit, which still glowed with embers. They sat on the dew-dampened grass. Rush sipped the coffee while she ate her noodles.

A few minutes later, Shook, Rider and Stoke joined them, each accepting a cup of the black brew. Rider and Stoke appeared about as sluggish as Rush. She doubted they'd be leaving today. Clearly, the men needed to recover before driving.

"Did you seek answers about Malika?" Shook asked his father.

White Wolf nodded. "Feather Blue is torn between darkness and light. There is a strong force in her life which binds her like chains on a slave. I could not discern this force."

Shook seemed completely alert. "What about the white lines on her face?"

"She has connected her spirit to yours, my son. This is very dangerous. Her aura is dark, yet conflict weighs heavily on her heart. In such a place, a soul can be lost...or found. I could not see her future, only her past."

"Can you tell us what you saw?" Cameo asked hesitantly, not wanting to seem impatient.

"Two men," White Wolf began, "captured and tortured Feather. They took her babes then sent her away. Her heart darkened. She drifted into cloaked spirit worlds, gathering allies from evil sources. A root of bitterness took hold in her soul sending her on a quest for revenge. That is never a good path."

"I agree," Cameo said. "I've had to work hard to forgive those who hurt me."

"The path of peace is always best, it leads to light. Feather is reaching out but unsure of who to trust, or if redemption is even possible for her," he told them, then shifted his focus to Shook. "She will follow you unless you cut her off."

"How do I achieve that?" asked Shook.

"On a vision quest. You can summon the white buffalo to sever the ties Feather has initiated with you."

"What will happen to her if I pursue the separation?" Concern hung on his voice, which surprised Cameo.

"I don't know. For some reason, she's clinging to you...and reaching for her daughter." White Wolf sighed. "I sense her intent is not evil in this case, only confused. However, do not mistake me, her discord can lead to treacherous consequences. If you choose to try and help her, arm yourself with wisdom and faith. And even that may not be enough."

"Yeshua," she murmured, wondering how the ancient name for Jesus came to her mind.

"The white man's God." White Wolf lowered his brows in open disapproval.

"No." Cameo refuted. "All man's God. There is no color or

race, no sinner that Yeshua would refuse." She caught the guys exchanging apprehensive looks. "Are none of you man enough to agree with me? Rush? You wear a cross around your neck. You saw the Hispanic angel girl." Then she turned a heated gaze on Shook. "Are you men of faith or not?"

"We are," Shook replied. "We just avoid discussing religion. It's a hot topic."

"Rush?" She looked to him again. "Do you feel the same?"

"I believe in God," he replied. "But in the work we do, we can't force our personal beliefs on others. We rescue people from all walks of life. Many of them don't believe. Others have different ideas concerning God, such as White Wolf here. He worships the Great Spirit. We choose to respect everyone's beliefs."

Cameo pushed to her feet and tossed her empty container into the small fire. "I believe in God the Father, the Son and the Holy Ghost." She turned her head sharply toward Shook again. "Choose what you will. But if Malika is crying out for help, I'd rather trust my God to pull her through than cut her off in some drug induced vision quest." With that she stomped away toward the bikes.

Sitting on the back of Rush's Harley, she pulled the blue feather from her jacket and stared at it. "Malika...or whatever your name is, if you're trapped between worlds, I won't abandon you."

Rush approached. "Is that from your mother?" he asked.

She nodded. "I'm sorry I didn't tell you. Her appearances have frightened me."

"You seemed utterly blissful last night dancing with her," he pointed out.

"Yes. That was an incredible experience. But her first two visits were uncertain and came with warnings."

"Two?" He arched a brow.

"In the motel, when I went back in for the jacket, there was a trail of blue feathers on the floor that led to the bathroom. I had to follow it. Malika appeared and told me that Rebar was trapped in his car from the storm, so I messaged Moss."

"Whoa, you never let on all this time."

"Sorry."

"Has Moss confirmed this?"

"No. But we may be out of cellphone range."

Rush looked down at the ground with a slow shake of his head. "Not sure what's going on with you, angel. But I've noticed a change since Malika appeared. Maybe White Wolf is right. Maybe her connection is dragging you down."

"That's rather judgmental, don't ya think?"

"Considering everything she's done? No."

Cameo felt suddenly alone. Rebar had never condemned her mother. He simply jumped into the fight at her side with faith and never second-guessed his decision. If only her sister hadn't got in the way.

"I'm going to find out what dark force has bound my mother. She's obviously reaching for help." Cameo lifted the fragrant shawl to her nose. "And she's chosen me to help her."

"Baby," Rush protested. "Of course she's zeroed in on you. You're the nice twin. Camille only helps herself."

"Then maybe it's my calling to pull Malika out of whatever darkness she's trapped in." She stared Rush straight in the eyes. "She left me a single feather for protection, then a trail of feathers to warn me. Last night, White Wolf summoned her spirit into the dance. I get that she's done horrible things. But you heard Shook's father...two men tortured her."

Frustration shadowed Rush's face. "Malika deliberately dragged you through hell on her warpath. And you're still willing to help her?"

"Ricochet was. Your family not once balked at rescuing her despite her past. You told me Ricochet doesn't judge. Isn't that what you're doing right now?"

"No. I'm trying to save you from going down the rabbit hole with her."

Cameo grew quiet and sat thinking hard over all the facts, and the ambiguities. Rush made valid points yet was clearly allowing his personal feelings to dictate his attitude. Their dispute regarding her mother could very well define their future together. Though Malika didn't seem to deserve forgiveness, Cameo couldn't help but wonder who drew those lines and when.

Not one person here was innocent. And weren't all sins the same? She called to mind what she knew about scripture. Since meeting Rebar, she'd started reading the Bible in her quiet moments. From what she understood, all people regardless of race, gender, or status in life, were offered redemption by the blood of Jesus Christ. He forgave murderers, prostitutes, and anyone who sincerely pleaded for mercy. His grace was a precious gift poured out to all who longed to receive it.

Surely, Yeshua would forgive my mother if she asked.

Cameo considered everything the Medicine Man had said. He possessed impressive insight and wisdom. Yet he seemed to lack compassion. He'd delivered facts and advice without emotion. Even more unsettling, he'd used drugs to confuse the men while he lured Malika from hiding.

She looked up at Rush who now straddled his seat facing her. "Doesn't it bother you that the old man laced the marijuana with peyote to perform his unorthodox ritual?"

Rush sighed and shrugged. "Yeah...I guess. Really wiped us out. Even so, I still saw you dancing with her. I was high, yet strangely aware."

"All four of you were trashed. What if I had needed help? I don't know where I am. I don't have my car. There's no cellphone service..." She kept tapping her phone, hoping to hear from Moss. "And some ancient old man led us into a ritual we knew nothing about. I thought we were just coming up for answers."

"I'm sorry," he said. "You're right. We put you in a vulnerable position. You don't seem worse for wear, though. And I'm not convinced it was a hallucination. You have the shawl."

She slanted a confused look at him. "I do, don't I. So, the old man found a way to get Malika here. She was really here. We *did* dance together. It wasn't just in my head." She let out a huff. "See what I mean? Even I'm befuddled and I wasn't high. And he did it in a way that protected Malika. You and Shook couldn't have captured her had you wanted to. Your minds weren't even your own."

"How could Malika get up here all the way from Dallas?" Rush seemed frustrated and confused.

"She could be following us. I saw her at the motel. Maybe that wasn't an illusion either. I did see the feathers on the floor."

"This is getting freaky," Rush admitted.

Shook wandered over to them. "Are you guys okay?"

"Just talking," she replied.

"I'm sorry my father offended you. He's very traditional and too old to change his ways," Shook told them.

"I don't blame *you*," Cameo said. "Last night was unlike anything I've ever experienced. Your father has unusual magic."

"Not magic," Shook refuted. "Medicine. He used herbs and natural elements of nature to achieve his goals. Did you get the answers you wanted?"

"Sort of. At least now we know why my mother has attached herself to you." Cameo tilted her head inquisitively. "What have you decided?"

Uncertainty glimmered in Shook's eyes. "My father feels strongly that if you choose to help Malika, you'll go down the dark path with her because you're her shadow child. He said she chose your name because she saw in you what he sees."

Cameo lifted her chin. "Then my destiny was established at birth. I am compelled to follow the path before me."

"You're going to help her after all she's done?" Shook's brows lifted.

"Wanna cuff me now?" Cameo scoffed, holding out her wrists.

His eyes widened slightly, then a grin hinted at his lips, turning those sweet corners into adorable dimples. "Nope. If you're willing to forgive her, I can't deny that level of grace. I've never seen it in anyone, and I've met a lot of people."

Cameo blinked in surprise. "You're not going to sever the connection she established with you?"

"I can't do that to you. If you believe there's hope in turning your mother away from darkness, in releasing her from whatever force binds her, then I'm in."

Rush gave his friend a sideways glance. "You're in love with Malika Rain?"

"In love?" Shook scoffed. "Nah. I just can't cut off her lifeline if she's trying to save herself."

"What about your badge?" Cameo asked.

Shook stepped over to her and draped an arm around her shoulders. "Halo...sometimes doing the right thing requires stepping outside the law."

CHAPTER SEVEN

Cameo sat near the bikes most of the day watching Shook reconnect with his father by helping with repairs to his cabin. Rush, Stoke and Rider worked alongside them. Thanks to no connection, she still hadn't heard from Moss and wondered if perhaps walking closer to the highway might help get reception to her phone.

The men seemed fully involved with their male-bonding, so she slipped away quietly and strolled down a path toward the road. She didn't feel afraid. Knowing more about her mother, and experiencing the dance, had instilled a renewed sense of courage in her spirit.

So when she spotted blue feathers on the walking trail, Cameo was not alarmed. Obviously, Malika had found a way to follow them and was trying to reconnect. She wondered though, how her mother had managed to travel all the way from Dallas to South Dakota. *Has someone helped her?*

The trail of feathers led her to a stream and stopped there. Cameo found a fallen tree to sit on. She gazed out over the wide stream. Rays of sunlight sliced through the treetops to cast an enchanting sparkle on the running water. She liked this spot and felt at home. She'd spent many days in various wildernesses around the globe. She never feared being alone with nature, well, except for severe storms.

Rustling in the brush caught her attention. She watched and waited.

"You came..." Malika crawled from the thicket yet appeared completely unscathed and immaculate as ever still wearing the feathered headdress, unique paint and black dress.

"Yes," Cameo responded softly. "Seems I've been following your feather trails lately."

A puckish smile hinted at her red painted lips. "It was the only way I could think of to get your attention."

"The blue smoke's an interesting touch as well. Are you into magic or something?"

Malika shook her head then knelt on the ground in front of Cameo. She sat back on her bare feet. "The Lakota spirit is strong in me. Always has been. I utilize nature to achieve my power."

"And just what power is that, Mother? Are you using it to bolster your thirst for revenge?"

"No."

"What do you want from us?" Cameo went straight to the point. "I've learned that you established a connection with Shook. Do you seek to harm him?"

Sadness glistened in Malika's eyes. "I am hurt by his betrayal...but no, I do not wish to harm him. I'm torn."

"How have you managed to follow me? You were in Dallas, then Lincoln, and now here. Are you a figment of my imagination? I'm struggling with this whole road trip."

"I had someone drive me. We were able to catch up when you stopped for the night."

"Who brought you?" she demanded. "Who is helping you?"

"Did you check on Rebar?" she asked without answering the question.

"I did but haven't heard back from Moss yet. That's why I took a walk, hoping for reception on my phone."

"Check your phone again."

Cameo cast her a puzzled look but pulled her phone out anyway. The device began pinging repeatedly as unread messages came through. "Oh my gosh. I've reentered civilization." She read through the texts. "You were right. Rebar and Chamber got caught in the tornado and were trapped. Moss and Levi found them. Moss said nobody was seriously hurt but Rebar's car is trashed." She looked at Malika. "How'd you know?"

"I was born with the gift of premonition. It's not evil and it has nothing to do with witchcraft. It's just a gift the spirit world bestowed upon me."

"You saved Rebar's life. Who knows how long he and Chamber would've been trapped had you not told me?" Tears misted her eyes.

"You still love him."

Cameo averted her gaze toward the stream. "It doesn't matter now."

"He still loves you so much, darling. Can you not forgive him or forgive me for pushing Camille in his face?"

"Why, Mother? Why were you so cruel that day?" Cameo asked without looking up.

"Shade," her mother replied. "I'm involved with Shade."

Cameo's gaze snapped back to her mother. "What?"

"You weren't in America during the Louisiana abduction. I sent Camille after Shade, thinking he'd be the perfect match for her. And for a while he was." She paused then sighed. "Until Shade came looking for me."

"Shade pursued *you*?" Cameo gasped in shock. "I thought it would be the other way around."

Malika nodded. "Apparently our brief encounter at the compound stuck in his mind. Perhaps I'm to blame. I was rather flirtatious while he was chained to the pole. But I never thought he'd take me seriously, let alone track me down."

Cameo shook her head to clear her mind. "He'd never do that. You killed his brother Dale, and you were enemies with Shade's favorite person."

"Ah, you speak of that evil bastard, the General."

"How could Shade, who was crazy in love with Camille, get past all that and go after you?" Cameo began to doubt her mother's outrageous story.

"Never ever underestimate the power of a woman," Malika stated in her typical no-nonsense manner. "Or the lust of a man."

"Is that why you tried hooking Camille up with Rebar again?"

Malika's expression deepened. "That was Shade's idea. His anger toward Rebar over betraying the General is inconceivable. He wants to know how Rebar found the old coot's location. And...Shade wants me. He devised the plan to set Camille up with Rebar and have us search his office to find the tracking device. We were to bring it back so Shade could tamper with it. Shade figured his plan would accomplish two things, get Camille out of our way, and thwart Rebar's efforts."

Cameo was at a loss for words. She gawked at Malika, utterly perplexed. They sat in silence while Cameo struggled to sort her thoughts. Everything her mother just said lined up with the why and how of what she and Camille had done. There was a missing piece, though, her twin's willingness to participate.

"Does Camille know of your affair with her fiancé?"

"No. And she should never know."

"Why?"

"Because she's pregnant with Shade's child," Malika told her.

"Oh, no!" Cameo gasped again. "But he's in love with you."

"Many men have been in love with me. However, I am not in love with Shade."

Cameo stared with a probing look. "Then why on Earth are

you having an affair with him?"

"I thought I was in love with him," she confessed. "It was the first time in my life I felt anything other than contempt toward a man. Shade was sweet, gentle, and a hunk of man any woman would love to have in her bed."

"So, what happened? Why aren't you in love with him anymore? Is it because Camille's pregnant? Which totally blows my mind by the way." Cameo could barely grasp any of this. She was glad Shook had warned her off the laced marijuana last night. "Oh...I get it, you fell for Shook. That's why you latched onto him."

"No, darling. Though I will admit Shook is easy on the eyes."

Cameo blew out a frustrated breath. "Then just tell me, Mother, what's going on? You obviously felt something for Shade to sleep with the man after using such extreme measures to get him and Camille together in the first place. Why would you give him up after going to all that trouble? Is it because Rebar and Camille didn't get back together as you and Shade hoped? Do you feel sorry for her? What? What are your reasons?"

"No, no, no." Malika shook her head vehemently, causing the colorful feathers of her headdress to undulate around her face. "Shade wants me but will soon discover he's bound to his fiancée in a way he can never let go. Camille doesn't know who she wants but she has no choice now. Honestly, darling, I'm not sure you can handle this truth. I fear how it may affect you."

Cameo bristled at the ominous shadows in Malika's eyes. She recognized those ghosts. "Please don't tell me the General survived that mess in Amarillo, or that you fired blanks and faked his death like Joan faked hers. Please, Mother, please don't tell me that evil beast still lives...please..." Her voice cracked as she fought the urge to break down.

"No, my sweet one, I would never do that to you. I emptied my gun into the General. He and Missy are surely gone from this world never to threaten you again." Malika reached out and held Cameo's hand. "However, there is a man we never considered who may pose a problem for us."

"Who?" She couldn't grasp what Malika was trying to spill. "Stop talking in circles and tell me."

Malika drew a deep breath then exhaled. Her eyes met Cameo's straight on. Her voice was still delicately soft yet steady as she replied, "His son. The General has a son."

Her mind raced. She did a quick mental backtrack. "But he was sterile."

"That's what I thought, too," Malika said. "Until I overheard something not meant for my ears. The General fathered a son to another woman before his war accident, before he met me...a son whose paternity was concealed."

Cameo couldn't fathom that a piece of her abuser lived on. "And Shade found the son and recruited him into his troop. That's why you lost your feelings for him, isn't it?"

"Now you see why I cannot love Shade. I could never love anyone related to that evil General."

"Related? Shade is related to the devil's son?" Her thoughts tumbled. "He has another half-brother? That makes Rebar—" She stopped short and clasped a hand over her mouth. "Oh no. No. No. No," she muttered in muffled disbelief behind her hand. The thought of Rebar and Rush bearing even the slightest connection to that man horrified her.

She felt her world falling apart.

"You're getting ahead of me," Malika said. "Nadia is the woman who birthed the General's only offspring. Dale was the only half-brother to his son."

Cameo stared at her mother with wide eyes. Her hand dropped to her side. "Shade? Shade is the General's son?"

Malika nodded. "He doesn't know that I know. Nobody

does. We must keep this between us. If he believes his secret is safe, then I am also safe. Your instincts were strong, *Shadow of our ancestors...*"

Cameo's thoughts unraveled. "Is this why you're after Shook? You're starting all over again? You want Shook to help you destroy Shade?"

"No!" Emotion flooded her riveting eyes. "Well, mostly no. I reached out to Shook as a lifeline. I'm terrified, Cameo. I want out of Shade's life. Very soon he will find out Camille is pregnant. He'll be forced to make the honorable choice and cut me loose to save his reputation. His men don't know of his affair with me. He'll make sure they never do."

"Are you sure the child is his?" She stiffened over the fact that Rebar could be the father.

"I am certain. Camille is almost three months along. She cannot hide it much longer."

Cameo considered her mother's recent state of mind and asked, "How did you learn of Shade's paternity? Are you certain the source was reputable?"

"I was about to drop in for a tryst when I heard Shade speaking with Jackson about his father. He sounded overly upset. Naturally, my curiosity piqued so I waited on the porch and eavesdropped. He'd just received the call informing him of the General's death. I could not believe my ears when he referred to the man as his father. I listened to the entire conversation just to be sure I wasn't hearing it wrong. Sure enough, the General was his father," she explained with shakiness in her voice. "I silently turned around and left."

Cameo sighed despondently. "Does he know you pulled the trigger?"

"No. He told Jackson that Ricochet killed his father. But don't worry, he can't go after them since Camille told him Shook is a Federal Agent. Shade is more focused on concealing *his own* identity than anything else."

"That explains Shade's unwavering loyalty and strong attachment to the Military. But why would he let that man hold you captive?"

Malika gave a light shrug. "To protect our affair. He'd never taint his reputation by letting anyone discover he was unfaithful. I wasn't the General's prisoner for long, thanks to you. I knew you'd search for me. He grabbed me that night after you and I had dinner."

"I knew something was wrong when I couldn't get in touch with you. Rebar was the only one who cared. Then Chamber got onboard and brought in Ricochet." Cameo studied her mother's face. "What do you want with Shook? I care about him. He's become a good friend. He's half Lakota, too."

"Ah, so that's why I was able to establish a connection with him. He's an intriguing man. I won't hurt him. But I fear he'll take me into custody if he gets the chance."

"I'm not so sure about that," Cameo said. "He seems to have a soft spot for you."

"Someone's coming," Malika whispered suddenly. "I must go."

"You still haven't told me who drove you up here." She quickly assessed the possibilities and hoped it wasn't Shade.

"Your sister brought me. She wanted to go for a drive to tell me the news of her pregnancy. She understands how your friends feel about her. She opted to wait a safe distance away."

"I see. I'm surprised she agreed to help you. I don't understand her."

"Her life is changing in a big way. Shade will never let her go now. She's having his son...I'm sure you can comprehend the ties that bind."

"How do you know she's having a baby boy?" Cameo slanted a puzzled look.

"I received a vision."

She didn't bother to inquire further. The Lakota spirit

world was a mystery to her. "Sadly, Camille has sealed her future to the wrong man."

"Sad for Camille but a fortunate break for me," Malika confessed. "I will be free of Shade's pursuit. This conversation must forever stay between us, and only us."

"I understand."

"Thank you," Malika said with a sigh of relief.

"Mother...do you believe in God?"

Malika placed her dainty hands upon Cameo's knees and gazed up at her with radiant eyes. "I believe whatever you believe, my shadow daughter. If you've found forgiveness in your heart toward me, then your God...is my God."

"I do forgive you." Cameo wrapped her fingers around Malika's.

"Stay one more night," Malika implored with a grateful smile. "Dance with me again tonight."

Before Cameo could respond, her mother vanished, leaving a faint blue mist in her place. A blue feather drifted down from out of nowhere. She caught it in midair and hugged it to her chest. Though she didn't understand everything, she felt in her soul that Malika had spoken the truth.

Most importantly, she comprehended White Wolf's words. *Feather Blue is torn between darkness and light. There is a strong force in her life which binds her like chains on a slave. I could not discern this force.*

The Medicine Man hadn't been able to discern the force binding her mother, but Cameo just did. Perhaps Malika didn't trust the old Indian enough to reveal this to him. She believed her mother possessed powerful medicine of her own, or as Malika had put it—premonition. Whatever her gifts, they were enough to keep others from prying into her secret thoughts.

She sat on the log, replaying the conversation in her head. Though Malika had played a painful role in the breakup with Rebar, she hadn't orchestrated it, as Cameo initially thought.

Cameo found some solace in that. Still, Rebar had succumbed to her twin's seductive wiles. However, he showed intense remorse. She couldn't deny that she missed him and was greatly relieved he hadn't been badly hurt in the storm.

Crunching footsteps caught her attention. She swung her legs around on the log to see Rush tromping through the thicket.

"What are you doing down here?" he asked. "Are you upset that we got busy helping White Wolf?"

"No. I decided to take a walk through nature and see if I could get reception on my phone."

"And did you?" He arched questioning brows.

"Yes. All my unread messages came through." She handed him her phone. "Malika was right. Thank goodness I texted Moss so they could find the guys."

Rush read the messages and nodded in agreement. "Amazing. Your mother may have saved their lives." He handed her phone back. "You're holding a new feather. I take it she found you again?"

Cameo nodded. "She seems different. Humble. Real. We had a good talk. She asked me to stay one more night to dance again."

"Well, I don't think you'll get any argument from us. The old Medicine Man worked us hard. I think we've completely rebuilt his cabin," Rush scoffed in jest.

"How'd you know where to find me?" she asked. "I could've gone in any direction."

Rush smiled then gently pulled her to her feet. "I followed the trail of feathers."

CHAPTER EIGHT

Cameo marveled over Malika's visit and how she'd allowed Rush to see the feathers and find her. It was almost as if she'd waited until they'd had time to finish their talk before letting anyone interrupt. She began to believe her mother truly did possess the gift of premonition, or intuition, or something to that effect. Whatever it was, it was powerful Native medicine...

She'd never been superstitious or believed in any type of magic. But nature was at times incomprehensible and if her mother's gift was an innate blessing, then she would not speak against it.

Their intimate conversation was nothing short of earth-shattering. Her twin carrying the General's grandson. Horrible news. And her mother's clandestine affair with Shade was appalling. Cameo was aghast that Shade pursued his fiancée's mother. Regardless, his world would soon be blown apart.

She wondered how Malika knew the baby's gender. Maybe her mother's uncanny intuition truly was on target. Cameo couldn't envision much of a future with her sister after hearing all this. She doubted her ability to even look at Shade's son and not quiver. The General's lineage lived on through Shade, which on the upside meant he was not a Damocles man. This would be significant news to Rush if only she could tell him. Rebar too, would be happy to know.

Nevertheless, she wouldn't endanger her mother by breaking her trust. The last thing she wanted was for Shade to have a reason to stalk her or Malika like the General had done.

No. This secret must remain buried. And despite the gravity of the situation, I'm not one to judge. Shade ignited a chain reaction of sordid affairs that caused pain for too many people. Maybe one day, Rebar and Rush will discover the truth, but it won't be from me. Only God can handle something of this magnitude.

Yet even in the midst of these new shocking revelations, one question hovered in the back of Cameo's mind—could she trust Malika? Rebar had said it well to Camille...*fool me once.* Cameo contemplated telling Shook. *If anyone has the right to know—he does.*

The guys were onboard spending another night at White Wolf's cabin. Though a bit of tension lingered between Cameo and the Medicine Man, Shook was enjoying this precious time with the man who'd raised him, and White Wolf now could freely call him *son.*

She spent the afternoon picking blackberries from an abundant patch behind the cabin once the guys had cleared an access path. Rush hiked up to a river with his buddies to fish for dinner. She was relieved they'd enjoy fish tonight instead of chewy meat.

Spending time with an authentic Lakota man in his uncomplicated life felt refreshing. Cut off from the hustle bustle of the mainstream, White Wolf's lifestyle offered a sense of peace and oneness with nature—something Cameo hadn't been able to enjoy in months.

"You are a natural with Mother Earth," White Wolf told her as he approached with another bucket. "Do you mind if I help pluck the berries? The men are still fishing, and I would enjoy your company."

She smiled and sighed with relief. "I'm honored that you want to spend time with me. I'm sorry I got upset over our religious differences. I've never been judgmental. Lately, there's been a lot of emotions to deal with."

"I understand, *Shadow Dove*," he said with a smile that spread to his eyes, eyes that shone with vitality despite his age.

"Shadow Dove?" She tilted her head curiously.

"I've been praying all day for wisdom," he told her. "The Great Spirit gave me your Lakota name. Do you like it?"

"Yes." She laughed a little. "Not sure the guys can handle another name, though. They call me Halo. Others call me by my birth name, Cameo."

"They can still call you Halo." He smiled. "But I will always know you as Shadow Dove. Do you know why?"

She nodded. "Because I am the shadow of my Lakota heritage."

"And because you seek peace in all things. Your spirit animal is the dove. I am pleased that you have accepted your Lakota birthright though you were raised in the white man's ways."

"I've lived in many parts of the world and have met many cultures. I was always careful not to disrespect their faith."

White Wolf hung his head. "As I did to you. For that I am sorry. A Tribal Elder once told me, only a foolish man thinks he is too wise to listen to others."

"Apology accepted." She offered her hand as a sign of peace.

"Your spirit is burdened today," he remarked.

"Perhaps just a little," she said. "I'll be okay. Sometimes, there are matters a woman must sort on her own."

He rustled in the bushes toward an unpicked patch of ripe plump berries. "A woman who holds her tongue is worth much. I see why the men call you Halo and why my son is very fond of you."

"Oh, Shook and I are only friends. I'm dating Rush," she informed him.

"Do not let new love make you blind." He wiggled bushy brows at her. "You are half Lakota as is my son. One never knows how the spirits will lead."

She let out a short uneasy laugh. "I am certain we are just friends."

"Hm." White Wolf muttered without looking up. "Seems my son trusts you very much to bring you here. Trust is a valuable gift not to be disregarded."

She sensed his intuition zeroing in on her torn emotions. He didn't want Shook to be ambushed by Malika. Was her request for another dance a ploy to draw on Shook's sympathy? As always, Malika brought mystery to the table wherever she went.

"My bucket is full," she told him, then walked away. She felt his eyes burning into her back. *Powerful Lakota spirits,* she mused.

Shook was preparing wood for the night's fire when she approached the front yard of the cabin.

"Where are the others?" she asked him.

"Fishing. Father told them not to return emptyhanded," he replied with a grin, then held up his string of fish.

"I bet you've had more practice than they have," she teased.

He laughed. "Yep. White Wolf taught me everything in my youth about living off the land."

She sat down on a nearby rock. "Can we talk before the guys come back?"

He glanced at her then laid the sticks aside. "Sure, babe. Everything okay?"

"I've been wrestling with this all day," she began, patting the ground beside her. "Your father seems to read minds."

"Did he offend you again?"

"No not at all," she quickly replied. "I got the impression he thinks there's something between you and me."

Shook plopped down beside her and stared toward the woods. "He's old."

"Maybe he senses your uncertainty toward Malika?" She

took a guess.

"Better talk faster, Halo. Our friends weren't far behind me in their quest for fish," Shook told her.

"I saw her today."

"I know."

Cameo slanted him a probing look. "Rush told you?"

"No. Have you forgotten so quickly I am also Lakota? I felt her presence. When you returned, I saw the new feather you tried to hide."

"Oh." Sudden awkwardness washed over her.

He swung his legs around to straddle the rock she sat upon and rested his arms on bent knees, then made unsettling eye contact with those black eyes. "Well?"

"Wow..." She blew out a breath. "You don't mess around." Flutters filled her beneath his heated gaze. "There's a lot to tell but I'll give you this. Camille and Malika have been following us. Malika and Shade are secretly involved but now she wants out because some disturbing facts have come to light." Cameo chose to omit Shade's shocking paternity to protect her mother. "I think Malika has her sights set on you, but she was vague about why. Shade and his guys know you're a Federal Agent."

"I kinda figured Camille would tell them," he said, unfazed, then asked, "What disturbing facts would cause Malika to give up her boytoy?"

"I don't even know how to say this. I'm not even sure I can utter the words again." She began to tremble. She didn't want to break Malika's confidence, yet she also didn't want to keep secrets from Ricochet.

Conflict tormented her soul.

"Hey..." he murmured, then slid to his knees and pulled her into his arms. "Don't go to pieces on me here, babe."

"Shade is the General's son," she muttered against his neck before the courage to do so left her. "And Camille is pregnant with Shade's offspring."

"Malika told me the General couldn't father kids due to a war accident."

"Apparently, before his war accident, he did have a child with Nadia."

Shook didn't move, didn't speak for a timeless moment Cameo knew neither would forget as they absorbed a new terrifying reality.

When Cameo composed herself, she told him, "Malika asked me to dance with her again tonight."

Shook pulled back to look at her. "She's challenging you."

"What?" Her eyes widened.

"Her Lakota Medicine is more powerful than we thought. She's Feather Blue."

"I'm not following you."

He took both her hands in his and sat back on his knees. "She's using her Lakota name to summon dark spirits and enhance her power. I know you don't like the term magic, but Feather Blue is Native American magic at its worst."

"Worse? I thought she sounded better!" Cameo cried. "She seemed remorseful and honest. She even said my God is her God if I could forgive her."

"I'm glad you told me this before it was too late." His eyes shimmered with emotion. "Tonight, enter the dance. I will join in and protect you. Together, we can drive back her dark spirit, and hopefully, separate Malika from the dark force binding her. If she refuses to detach herself from evil, I will have no choice but to dissolve the connection she's trying to make with me."

"I have no Lakota power. How can I possibly be of help?"

He cupped her chin with a gentle hand and stared into her eyes. "You have Yeshua. I will subdue her Lakota magic while you pray to the ultimate power."

"You're a Christian?"

"Yes. I suppose I'm quiet about my faith because of my line of work. But it lives strongly in my heart. Father reacted to your outspoken nature, not your belief in God," he told her. "In his world, women are not permitted to speak on spiritual matters."

"My mind is reeling." She didn't think she could handle much more, yet she wouldn't let him down. Despite her fear of Malika's trickery, she'd enter the circle tonight with Shook. "Please don't tell anyone Shade is the General's son until my mother is safe." She stared at him with pleading eyes, feeling horribly guilty for spilling the secret already. But something about Shook inspired trust. "I confided in you because White Wolf knew I was holding back. And...because I care about you. I don't want Malika to trick you."

He knelt before her, framing her face with gentle hands. "The secret is safe with me. We'll reveal this when the time is right." His lips touched hers, fleetingly, but with evident affection. "My father was not so far from the truth, hm?"

She quivered beneath his potent allure, completely lost for words. Shook flashed an engaging smile then eased back.

"If anyone can pull Malika from the dark world she's lost in, it is you. I've never met anyone with a more forgiving heart." He brushed a sweet kiss along her cheek. "Don't ever change, Halo."

CHAPTER NINE

Splinters of light shifted over the trees as the sun slowly dropped from the sky. Hues of gold and blue radiated around the cabin. Cameo had remained quiet most of the day, half-fretting, and half-praying over tonight's dance. She'd found flour and sugar in White Wolf's makeshift pantry to bake a blackberry cake on his woodburning stove.

She did everything she could to take her mind off Malika's intense visit and then the equally intense moment with Shook. Why he'd kissed her went beyond her comprehension. He was Rush's best friend. And his remark afterward left her wondering about these men. They didn't appear to respect boundaries.

Chamber had made a move the day Rebar dumped her. Rush blatantly stated his intent while she was still with Rebar. And now Shook mesmerized her with a touch of his lips and a few sensually whispered words.

Rush hadn't said much, which made her worry. He spent the afternoon cleaning fish and helping prepare the fire for cooking. White Wolf stuffed the fish with wild vegetables from his little garden and coated them with soybean oil. They wrapped the fish in foil and laid them on a metal rack once the flames died down.

While the fish cooked, Rush sat with her. "I saw you and Shook having what seemed like a serious conversation today. I didn't want to interrupt so I went about some chores. But can you tell me about it?"

"We talked about my visit with Malika," she replied. "I

wasn't going to tell anyone what she revealed to me, but White Wolf sensed I was holding out and he made it clear that breaking Shook's trust would be disrespectful."

"Ah, Indian matters, huh?" he teased with a wink.

She shrugged. "Something like that."

"I gotta admit this trip hasn't been one of my more enjoyable ventures. I've had zero time alone with you and when we are alone, you're still miles away."

"I'm sorry. I never anticipated any of this when I mentioned seeking answers."

"And did you find them?" he asked.

"More than I ever bargained for." She sighed and looked up at him as they sat on the ground. "Tonight's dance may be extreme. I can't tell you everything I know right now."

"But you were able to confide in my best friend?"

"I had no choice. Would you rather I let your friend be ambushed by Malika?"

Mixed emotion lined his face. "You've been a closed book lately. First about texting Moss and now this. Who are you tonight...Halo or Shadow Dove?"

"You know the name White Wolf gave me?"

Rush arched his brows incredulously. "All the men are raving over it. You've made quite a splash up here in this Native world."

She didn't break eye contact while pondering his intrusive question. "Tonight...I must be both. Please don't be angry. Malika has targeted Shook, and we suspect she may be trying to use me to deepen her connection. I'm trying to protect your best friend."

"I could never be angry with you, angel. The way you extend yourself to help others in any situation sets you apart from anyone I've ever known." He caressed her face then filtered her hair through his fingers. "I love that about you."

She closed her eyes, basking in the comfort of his touch.

Their journey had been grueling with very little physical comfort. "Thank you," she responded in a whisper. "I never expected Malika to show up after what she did in Amarillo. I want to tell you everything, but I feel it would be best coming from Shook. I already feel guilty for breaking my mother's confidence to Shook, but I had moral reason to. I'm sure he'll fill all of Ricochet in. I just don't want to be the one they hear it from."

"Wow, babydoll, this must be serious." He held her tenderly. "You're shaking."

"Rush..." She breathed out his name and fell into his embrace. "You have no idea. But tonight needs to happen so we know where all the players stand."

"Okay, angel. Calm down. I didn't mean to upset you."

She eased from his arms. "We should join them. I think dinner's ready, and I don't want to make White Wolf growly."

"I hope you enjoy the fish better than the turkey," he said with a wink.

"It smells good. Not sure I can eat much. My nerves are on edge."

"We're here with you." He touched her cheek with the back of his hand. "You're safe, okay?"

She nodded. They strolled to the fire hand in hand. Everyone was chowing down by the time they plated their food.

"You guys caught a ton of fish," she remarked, staring at all the elongated foil wraps on the fire.

"They had a good hunt," White Wolf said with a pleased smile.

"Just fishing," added Rider. "Halo's not fond of hunters."

She offered Rider a grateful smile while picking at the fish. A mix of squash, corn and tomatoes was stuffed inside. The flesh was tender and flavorful but riddled with tiny bones. Apparently, the men hadn't taken the time to filet the fish. She ate what she could without complaint.

Stoke finished first and started throwing larger chunks of wood onto the fire. Shook and White Wolf retreated to his cabin. The Medicine Man returned with a handheld drum. The frame looked wooden, and she didn't want to know what the rest was made of for fear they'd butt heads again. He sat cross-legged on a stump near the fire.

"You aren't dancing?" she asked.

"No. Tonight you dance with my son to draw Feather Blue into the light."

A stiff breeze whipped her hair back. She looked around nervously and pulled the shawl tighter around her shoulders.

She did a doubletake when Shook emerged from the cabin bared to the waist wearing only threadbare jeans. Black paint was streaked crosswise upon his muscular chest in thick lines as if he'd dipped his fingers in paint and haphazardly dragged them over his skin. Red paint zigzagged down the center of his torso to his navel. On his face, three lines of white began near the bridge of his nose and stretched horizontally across each cheek to the outer edge of his high cheekbones.

Wow. She tried not to gawk, but he looked every bit the fierce warrior.

White Wolf began beating the drum and chanting in what she presumed was Lakota. Shook took her hand and led her to the fire. He began dancing in small circles so she followed his lead, knowing that Malika would soon appear. Even if her mother had considered changing her mind, she'd not be able to resist Shook's Native call.

They danced around the fire several times before Cameo found her rhythm and began to relax. Rush, Stoke, and Rider — all sober tonight, looked on in visible fascination.

White Wolf began to sing louder when blue feathers swirled from seemingly nowhere and settled in a circular breeze around Cameo. At that point, Shook took hold of her hand and laced their fingers together. Their eyes met — she was startled to receive his thoughts—the Lakota link between them seemed undeniably strong.

He silently told her that to draw the dark force out, Malika would need to be provoked. And nothing would incite her more than to think that Shook had feelings for her daughter. The thought whipped through her mind that perhaps this was his way of discreetly expanding upon the fleeting kiss she couldn't forget.

Cameo realized that Shook possibly knew Malika better than anyone here from the time he'd been undercover. She held his hand tightly, terrified to let go.

Not long after Shook took Cameo's hand, Malika entered the circle wearing the long black dress slit to her hip. A large floral tattoo adorned her thigh which she seemed to deliberately flaunt as if to draw attention to her sensuality. The rest of her appearance was the same as before, colorful paint, feathered headdress, and white markings.

A cunning smile curved Malika's vixen-red lips as she clutched Cameo's other hand. The dance intensified with each beat of the drum. They twirled and leapt, swayed, and gyrated, flinging their hair to the ancient rhythm of their ancestors.

Then Malika made her move. She brought her free hand in to pull Cameo and Shook apart. Shook turned his head sharply and glared at her, then gently shoved her back.

Malika made another attempt and was met with the same resistance. Her smile faded. Her black eyes took on a menacing glow and flames from the fire reflected in their depths.

Shook drew Cameo closer, tugging her free of Malika's grip. He wrapped both arms around her waist as they continued step-dancing around the circle.

Malika's true intent burst forth. She was not seeking forgiveness. She had chosen Shook as her next mate because she'd lost Shade.

Realizing that the dark force of Feather Blue had surfaced, Cameo began to pray. Her mother would either relinquish the dark spirit and truly seek forgiveness or she'd be driven back. Cameo grasped why Shook would need to sever the ties Malika had initiated if she didn't cooperate.

"Yeshua, bring your peace," Cameo sang softly. She watched Shook push Malika away numerous times.

White Wolf's chanting intensified, which Cameo sensed was prayer.

A tug of war ensued between her, Malika, and Shook but not the one she'd have expected. Instead of continuing her pursuit of Shook, her mother began tugging Cameo away from him as if to drag her from the circle — away from the protection of her friends.

Malika began repeating the same phrase in a language Cameo didn't understand. But by the tone in her voice, Cameo could tell the message was anything but repentance or a cry for peace.

Shook held her tightly, her back to his chest while Malika tried desperately to wrench her from his arms.

"Yeshua, your power reigns above all," Cameo prayed. "You defeated darkness. Conquered sin. Whatever force is here, I ask you to crush it now. I have no power on my own, Lord. But I know that there is power in your name. Yeshua bring your fire." She made eye contact with Malika. "Feather Blue," she cried out. "Choose who you will serve, darkness or light!"

At that, Malika gripped the shawl and yanked it from Cameo's shoulders. Anger flashed in her eyes followed by a flicker of challenge. She glanced at Shook then back at Cameo.

Shook shouted something in Lakota. His voice rang out above the roaring fire. He sounded fearless and unwavering.

Malika cowered at his words. She slunk back, balling the shawl into her fists. With a defiant shake of her head, she whipped the shawl into the fire. The fabric exploded into a fireball that shot into the night sky. Shook threw Cameo to the ground away from the circle and covered her with his body.

When she looked up, Malika was gone.

"Are you all right?" Shook asked.

"I-I think so." She flopped onto her back, staring up at him. "What happened?"

"She didn't get what she came for." He wasn't even slightly winded.

Rush and the others hurried to them. "Are you both okay?" he asked, brushing tangled hair from Cameo's face.

"I think so. That was terrifying." She pushed to a sitting position. "I take it Malika or Feather Blue didn't seek forgiveness."

"It was a trick," Shook told her. "She's been following you, showering you with praise and good deeds such as helping Rebar, gave you the shawl and even told you secrets to gain your trust. She's not ready to release the dark magic."

"We failed?" Cameo frowned.

"No. We drove her dark alter back and dissolved the link she'd begun to create between my spirit and hers. I suspect she initiated it during our time together while I was under-cover." He held her hand to his cheeks. "I felt the burden lift. The white lines are gone, aren't they?"

"Yes!" She gasped then exhaled a sigh of relief that something good had come from the ordeal.

"She is still dangerous," White Wolf warned them. "But you have saved my son, Shadow Dove. I am grateful."

Cameo smiled weakly. "Happy to help." Then she asked Shook, "What did you shout? Was that in Lakota?"

He nodded. "I told her that I don't love her. My heart is taken. And if I see her again, I won't be so generous."

"You'll arrest her?"

"Damn straight. She tried to take you right out from under

us. She is not Malika right now. I'm afraid her actions are being driven by Feather Blue," he told her.

"And Feather Blue's spirit is vindictive and callous," White Wolf added.

Cameo crawled into Rush's open arms. "Thank you for trusting us."

"Hey," he said in his naturally easy manner. "He's my best friend and you're my girl. I can see now why discretion was necessary." He glanced at Shook. "Can you tell us what's going on? Or is all this still undercover?"

Shook's gaze traveled around the gathering. He released a heavy sigh. "I think it's time we get everyone on the same page. Then we can dig deeper to see just how much of what Malika said is true."

Everyone gathered near the fire. Cameo sat between Rush and Shook, frequently glancing about for any sign of danger. Stoke and Rider took a seat across from them and White Wolf sat on his wooden tree stump.

"Halo shared some mind-blowing information with me today," Shook told them. "My cover is blown because Camille and Malika are with Shade."

"What do you mean Malika is with Shade?" asked Stoke. "As in intimately?"

Shook nodded. "They've been having an affair. I have a feeling war is coming."

"Shade's military. Even if he is shagging Malika, which is a disturbing thought, he'd never involve himself in her illegal activity," Rush disputed.

"I wouldn't underestimate him," said Shook. "There's more."

Cameo cast him a furtive glance, worried about revealing the ultimate secret too soon.

Shook glanced her way. Tension lined his face. "Shade has more to protect now, Camille is pregnant. And Malika will be in his way. The dynamics have shifted which makes them all ticking bombs."

Rush scoffed. "Are you sure it's Shade's? She was with Re-bar not so long ago."

"Thanks for the reminder." Cameo scowled. "But she's almost three months along. She wasn't with him then. I was."

"I see." A pensive look crossed Rush's face. "So that's why Malika is after Shook. She's about to lose her love interest."

"We're getting ahead of ourselves here," Stoke said. "What if we flip this around? Maybe Malika did all those nice things for you because she really does want your trust. From what I saw, she was trying to pull *you* away not Shook. Is it possible that Malika wants her other daughter, her Lakota daughter on her side because she'll soon lose Shade and Camille?"

His insight surprised Cameo. Stoke had always been one of the strong silent family members, like Rider. They were the dark horses in battle and solid backbones of Ricochet.

"Seems to me," Rush began after lengthy deliberation. "Once Malika realized a baby would end her fun with Shade, she set out to find a new support system. I'm getting the feeling that Malika doesn't like to play alone."

"You paint her out as a victim," Shook growled.

"Wasn't she?" argued Rush. "We know for a fact what those men put her through, and that her babies were stolen from her. What we don't know is when or how she drifted into darkness."

Cameo looked up at him. "Do you think there's still hope for her?"

"I don't know." Rush shrugged. "But Ricochet never judges. I've never dealt with legends or spirits, just facts and faith. You severed the ties she had with Shook." He gazed down at her, placing a gentle hand alongside her face. "I suggest we don't throw her to the wolves just yet. We need to definitely keep our guard up, especially where you and Shook are concerned. But let's see what her next move is. I really want to know the hard truth about Shade and Camille. We can't just take Malika's word on this."

"I agree with Rush," added Stoke. "If Malika is crying out for help, then we can't ignore her."

"So we handle it like all our other dangerous cases," Rider said. "Proceed with ultimate caution."

White Wolf stood and folded both arms across his chest. Lines on his face were taut, his eyes serious. "Only fools would show compassion to a dark spirit."

Shook stood and faced his father. "We intend no disrespect, Até, but these men have been my family all my adult life. I trust them. We rescue abused women. It's a different world now. I will be careful and keep my distance from Feather Blue so she cannot attach herself to me again. However, I cannot dismiss the wisdom of my friends. If we can save Malika and reunite mother and daughter, then it will be well worth the effort. Would you not chase a colt into a ravine to return it to the mare?"

"You play on my love for horses," White Wolf grumbled. "They are nature's glory. Feather Blue is not a horse."

"No. But she's my mother," Cameo said, standing up beside Shook. "All have fallen from grace at one point in their lives," she said with a knowing look.

White Wolf's expression softened. "Your heart is pure, Shadow Dove. I cannot deny your quest for peace. I shall pray to the Great One for safety and success in this path you have set your feet upon."

She inclined her head slightly. "Thank you, my friend."

A weathered smile tugged at his lips. "I sense you will be leaving with the morning sun. Let's enjoy the fire and finish the good food provided by Mother Earth before this night is through."

White Wolf resumed his spot on the stump. Rider, Stoke

and Rush remained seated. She figured they'd had enough drama for one night.

"I'm amazed at the effect you have on my father," Shook said with an incredulous expression.

"I think you paved the way. Thank you for what you said." She offered him a grateful smile. "And for what you didn't say," she added for only him to hear.

He gave her a wink. "I didn't think they could handle much more."

"I agree." She kissed his cheek as a gesture of appreciation then returned to sit with Rush. "Thank you for your unshakable leadership and compassion. Ricochet is incredible. The patience and wisdom I saw just now made me realize how fortunate I am to be part of this family."

Rush smiled. Pride and gratitude shone in his eyes. "Saving outcasts is how we got started. We won't deviate from our original purpose just because some spirits raise a fuss. I don't understand the Native American ways, but I respect their religion, as I do all beliefs. If we start picking and choosing who to rescue based on their faith, that's wrong and never what we want to be about."

"I love your stability," she said and let out a sigh of release.

Tonight had been anything but normal. She knew once they left this isolated camp, she'd second-guess all that had occurred.

Even so, she took comfort in the men around her, their strength and logic. They dug into the blackberry cake she made and showered her with compliments. She felt they were being overly nice to set her at ease, because she didn't think the cake turned out that great. Either way, she appreciated their thoughtfulness.

A waning crescent moon lingered high in the clear night sky amidst a billion twinkling stars. Cameo stood near the fire, keeping close to her family while gazing up at the enchanting slice of silver moon hovering overhead.

Before taking a bite of cake, she lifted her face toward the Heavens and closed her eyes. "Thank you, Yeshua, for helping us tonight. Please continue to guide us and cover us with your grace."

"Halo," Rush called in a gentle tone. "Come sit with us and relax, angel."

"Yeah, babe. We need to chill before hitting the road tomorrow," Shook chimed in.

She turned toward the men and smiled, then took a seat on the grass between them. Flames danced within the fire they'd built. Peace reigned over their circle for now. She embraced it with her heart, let it soak into her soul.

They'd won two battles but not yet the war.

However, she felt no fear. The rest of the night belonged to them, and she'd bask in the joy of defeating an evil spirit...if only for now.

She felt peace over their decision not to kick Malika to the curb yet as Shade would soon do. She didn't understand the compassion in her heart toward others at times. Nevertheless, she'd have it no other way.

Shook's discretion impressed her. He'd managed to tell their friends some of the new developments without overwhelming anyone. After all, they'd just witnessed an unforgettable spiritual battle moments before hearing that Malika and Shade were having an affair behind his pregnant fiancée's back.

She didn't think tonight at White Wolf's home was the right time or place to divulge all the details, and she agreed with Shook, the others couldn't handle much more right now.

"Everything okay?" Rush asked quietly.

She smiled and sighed contentedly while snuggling up to him. "Yeah. Tonight...everything is good."

Read what happens next in Feather Blue: Book 8

About the Author

Shiloh is a bookworm who grew into an author. Writing has been a way of life for her since grade school. In her words, "The only time I'm truly free is when I'm writing."

As a survivor of hardship and chronic disease, she takes one day at a time and treasures the simple things in life. Shiloh is a Christian, loves animals and practices being kind and generous every day.

Her achievements include The Golden Wings Award for her debut novel The Satellite, the UK Nobel Pin and Editor's Choice Award for her poem The Lonely Man, numerous 5 Star Reviews from Fallen Angels Reviews, InD'tale Magazine, and other professional reviewers for novels published under former pen names.

Her novel Forever in Darkness became a finalist in the 2017 RONE Awards.

Her novel *Chained Reaction* earned her third 5 Star Crowned Heart Review and a nomination for the RONE 2021 Awards.

Writing stories you'll live in!

www.SusanZoeBella.com